The innocent comment brought Lizzie to a halt. Could she handle Amanda's broken heart, and her own, when the time came and Hank left Kansas City? Lizzie prayed she would be able to. A small part of her dared to wish that day would never come. That Hank would stay.

"Come on, Mommy," Amanda cried, tugging on Lizzie's hand.

Over the top of her head, Hank gave Lizzie a look she had trouble identifying. A voice inside told her she was getting in too deep. But in fact, it was already too late.

She was falling in love with Hank Davis and there was nothing she could do to stop it....

Dear Reader,

Spring cleaning wearing you out? Perk up with a heart-thumping romance from Silhouette Romance. This month, your favorite authors return to the line, and a new one makes her debut!

Take a much-deserved break with bestselling author Judy Christenberry's secret-baby story, *Daddy on the Doorstep* (#1654). Then plunge into Elizabeth August's latest, *The Rancher's Hand-Picked Bride* (#1656), about a celibate heroine forced to find her rugged neighbor a bride!

You won't want to miss the first in Raye Morgan's CATCHING THE CROWN miniseries about three royal siblings raised in America who must return to their kingdom and marry. In *Jack and the Princess* (#1655), Princess Karina falls for her bodyguard, but what will it take for this gruff commoner to win a place in the royal family? And in Diane Pershing's *The Wish* (#1657), the next SOULMATES installment, a pair of magic eyeglasses gives Gerri Conklin the chance to do over the most disastrous week of her life...and find the man of her dreams!

And be sure to keep your eye on these two Romance authors. Roxann Delaney delivers her third fabulous Silhouette Romance novel, *A Whole New Man* (#1658), about a live-for-the-moment hero transformed into a family man, but will it last? And Cheryl Kushner makes her debut with *He's Still the One* (#1659), a fresh, funny, heartwarming tale about a TV show host who returns to her hometown and the man she never stopped loving.

Happy reading!

Mary-Theresa Hussey

Mary-Theresa Hussey
Senior Editor

Please address questions and book requests to:
Silhouette Reader Service
U.S.: 3010 Walden Ave., P.O. Box 1325, Buffalo, NY 14269
Canadian: P.O. Box 609, Fort Erie, Ont. L2A 5X3

A Whole New Man

ROXANN DELANEY

Published by Silhouette Books

America's Publisher of Contemporary Romance

If you purchased this book without a cover you should be aware that this book is stolen property. It was reported as "unsold and destroyed" to the publisher, and neither the author nor the publisher has received any payment for this "stripped book."

To Gail, who nudged me back to reading romance and knows me all too well. Thanks for believing in me more than I believe in myself and for being my best friend for more years than we need to count.

 SILHOUETTE BOOKS

ISBN 0-373-19658-X

A WHOLE NEW MAN

Copyright © 2003 by Roxann Farmer

All rights reserved. Except for use in any review, the reproduction or utilization of this work in whole or in part in any form by any electronic, mechanical or other means, now known or hereafter invented, including xerography, photocopying and recording, or in any information storage or retrieval system, is forbidden without the written permission of the editorial office, Silhouette Books, 300 East 42nd Street, New York, NY 10017 U.S.A.

All characters in this book have no existence outside the imagination of the author and have no relation whatsoever to anyone bearing the same name or names. They are not even distantly inspired by any individual known or unknown to the author, and all incidents are pure invention.

This edition published by arrangement with Harlequin Books S.A.

® and TM are trademarks of Harlequin Books S.A., used under license. Trademarks indicated with ® are registered in the United States Patent and Trademark Office, the Canadian Trade Marks Office and in other countries.

Visit Silhouette at www.eHarlequin.com

Printed in U.S.A.

Books by Roxann Delaney

Silhouette Romance

Rachel's Rescuer #1509
A Saddle Made for Two #1533
A Whole New Man #1658

ROXANN DELANEY

is the mother of four daughters. With the two oldest on their own, although a mere twenty yards away, life in her hometown in south-central Kansas is still far from dull. The 1999 Maggie winner enjoys keeping up with the former high school classmates she encounters and the tons of relatives, whose ancestors settled in the area over a century ago. A theater buff, she once helped establish a community theater and both acted and directed in the productions, as well as served on the board of directors. But writing is her first love, and she is thrilled to have followed the yellow brick road to the land of Silhouette Romance. She would love to hear from readers, who can write her at P.O. Box 636, Clearwater, KS 67026.

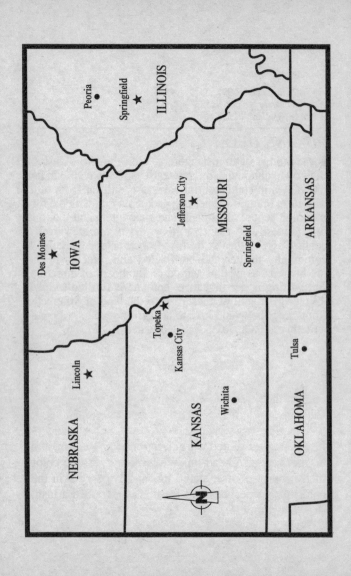

Chapter One

"Henry Davis?"

Hank looked up from the magazine he was thumbing through, and his breath lodged in his chest. Contacting this image-consulting place was one of the best ideas he'd ever had, considering the woman standing in front of him.

"I'm Hank." Disengaging himself from the chair, he rose to his feet.

Her smile was blinding. "Mr. Davis, I'm Elizabeth Edwards. Welcome to Kansas City and Images, Inc."

When he took the woman's outstretched hand in his, an unaccustomed warmth climbed up his arm, and he met her gaze head-on. Wide, blue eyes, the color of Navajo turquoise, stared into his. Smooth skin the color of ripe peaches and fresh cream framed a lush, strawberry mouth.

When he continued to stare, she pulled away with her breath-stealing smile intact. "Let's get comfortable in my office and discuss what it is specifically that I plan to do for you." She turned to her receptionist, robbing him of his view of her smile. "Perhaps Mr. Davis would like something to drink before we get started, Janine."

"I'm fine," Hank managed to say, even though he wasn't. He could've used a stiff drink as he studied her profile. When he'd seen the fancy ad in the Kansas City magazine back in New Mexico, he hadn't imagined he would encounter someone who looked like her. Not that he minded. He didn't know how long he would stay with his new foreman's job at Crown Construction, but he couldn't deny himself a few simple pleasures. That's as far as it would go, though. He had never been much of a ladies' man, and he knew better than to get tangled up with a woman. Most wanted to make things permanent and be a family—something he didn't know much about.

"We have a lot of things to accomplish, Mr. Davis," his new consultant said and motioned for him to follow her.

Hank had always believed a man had the right to take advantage of and enjoy things whenever the opportunity presented itself. Walking behind her down a hallway, that opportunity was a tantalizing view of a pair of curvy, swaying hips that hinted at what lay beneath the snug white skirt encasing them and a pair of long, shapely legs that stretched his imagination.

Shifting his gaze to rein in his fantasy, he barely noticed the pricey but tasteful decor of Images, Inc. as she led him to her office. Instead the alabaster column of her neck, revealed beneath a knot of gorgeous auburn hair, had snared his attention. Copper wisps escaped the bun and teased the collar of the virginal white suit she wore. His fingers itched to touch them and feel their silky softness. Too bad he would never get the chance to do it.

Before his imagination led him further than it should, they reached her office. She motioned toward a long sofa along one wall. While he took a seat, she picked up a file folder from her desk, then settled at the opposite end of the sofa. It didn't escape him that her skirt inched higher, revealing even more of her long legs, and he tried his best to ignore it so he could concentrate on the reason he was there.

After shuffling the papers in her hands, she looked up to give him another dazzling smile. "Tell me what convinced you to come to Images, Inc., Mr. Davis."

"Call me Hank." He crossed one work-booted foot over his knee and fingered a worn seam in the leather. The truth was, his thirtieth birthday three months ago had brought home the hard fact that he had never made much of himself. Then he had received the letter from Crown Construction offering him a position with the well-respected company. When he saw the ad for Images, Inc., he called on a whim, thinking he might as well give it a try and fill in the time during the next two weeks until he started his new job.

"I suppose you could say I thought I could use a little spiffing up," he said, giving away as little about himself as he could. "I could use a little polish, anyway. I've been on the road all my life, so I haven't picked up the social graces most people come by naturally."

She glanced at a paper, the bridge of her nose wrinkling in concentration. "You start a new job with Crown Construction in two weeks. You've been hired for a foreman position?"

He nodded. "I've been working construction for a

couple of years with the same company. With several other companies before that, too. Crown contacted me about the job. I'm not sure where they got my name, but I decided I might as well move up the ladder, since it was offered."

Her gaze met his, but she looked away quickly. "Let's go over your employment history, so I can get an idea of your experience."

He bit back a laugh. It had taken three extra typed pages to fill out his application for Crown. Thirteen jobs in as many years gave him more experience than most people, but he doubted this woman was interested in the details. "I worked the oil fields in Alaska, Oklahoma, and a short stint in Kuwait. I've been a ranch hand in Wyoming and Montana, a dockworker in San Diego, had a little rodeo here and there, worked on a salmon boat for a while out of—"

"I get the picture," she said and ducked her head to check the paper.

But not before he'd seen a flicker of something in her eyes. It passed too quickly to identify, so he chalked it up to nothing.

"Since you're so well-traveled," she said, meeting his gaze once again, "why did you choose Kansas City?"

Hank shrugged and focused on her question instead of her blue eyes. "Other than the fact that my mother was from here, Crown has a good reputation."

She picked up a pen and jotted something on the paper. "So you have relatives in the area?"

"Not that I know of."

"You don't know?"

"It's unlikely. My mother lost her folks when she was young. To be honest, I never heard her talk of any other family. I don't recall my dad talking about any family, either." Family wasn't all that important to Hank. He had been on his own, without any, for over ten years. Marriage and a family of his own weren't an option. Not for him. He had never had a permanent address other than a post office box and he didn't intend to change that. Not for long, anyway. Besides, he'd seen what a life of moving from one place to another had done to his mom. He wouldn't risk doing that to a woman he loved, and he wasn't going to change.

"Is your mother in New Mexico?" she asked, bringing his attention back to her.

"She died when I was ten."

Compassion shone in her eyes. "I'm sorry."

Wanting to ease her mind and curious to know about her, he turned the conversation around. "Do you have family here?"

She hesitated for a moment, then she nodded. "All but my dad."

This time he didn't miss the look in her eyes, and wondered at the sadness he saw there. The one thing he remembered about his mother was her telling him that the eyes were the windows to a person's soul. But it wasn't this woman's soul that he was interested in. Her looks had caught his attention, that was all.

"Well," she said, then cleared her throat. "Janine has the contract drawn up. We agreed on two weeks, right?"

"Right."

"We'll get started right away. Usually we work with a client for a minimum of a month. In your case, we'll have to be quick but thorough, with intense focus on the basics. Instead of a few hours a day, we'll work together most of the day, and occasionally into the evening. I hope you can block out the time, just for this."

"It's not a problem," he replied. Especially since he had nothing else to do until his job started.

Pulling a paper out of the folder, she placed it on top of the others and skimmed a long slender finger down it. "Our first order of business is to make sure you're living at an address that will reflect that you're a stable person. As they say in the real estate business, location is everything."

Her infectious grin caught him by surprise, and he wondered what lay beneath her cool exterior. "I have a room at the Regency out near the airport."

She shook her head, and he imagined that tight knot of hair at the back of her neck loose and flowing like a liquid flame. The thought made him want to reach out and start pulling out whatever held it in place, but he stopped the fantasy as soon as it started.

She offered a gentle smile. "In this case, since you'll be living here for some time, I think it's best to find something that could become more permanent."

"I don't know the area, but I'll trust your judgment," he said, thinking he might as well go along with her.

Flipping through a notebook, she stopped and made a note. "I know of an apartment that can be subleased. Even better, you can give it a try for a month before you make a decision."

Hank didn't plan to be in town long enough to need a permanent place to live and hoped he wouldn't get in over his head. He had the money, but getting out of a sublease could be tricky. Or at least that's what he'd heard. His usual trappings were more temporary.

Before he could voice his concern, the intercom buzzer sounded. "Excuse me," she said and walked to her desk where she leaned over to pick up the phone. "What is it, Janine?" She paused, listening. "I'll return her call later… Who? Did you get his number? Any idea— All right. Do what you can."

Replacing the receiver, she turned back to Hank. "I hate to rush you, but we might as well get started. If you'll stop at Janine's desk, she has the contract. Read it, make any changes you think are needed, then sign it. Do you have a car?"

He shook his head. "I left my pickup back in New Mexico. As soon as I landed, I dropped my things at the hotel and came straight here."

"No need to be in a hurry to get one. I can pick you up at your hotel in—" She glanced at her watch, frowning. "Two hours. That will give me time to make some arrangements on the apartment, and then we can decide where to go from there."

For some reason, she intrigued him. He wouldn't mind spending a little time with her. A little fun wouldn't hurt, either. There was no danger in that. But anything more was out of the question.

Standing, he took the hand she offered and held it. "Your friends call you Lizzie?"

She shook her head, but didn't pull away. "Professionally, I prefer Elizabeth."

"If it's okay with you, I'll stick with Lizzie."

"Well, I suppose—"

"Good. And I'm Hank."

Still holding her hand, he unconsciously rubbed his thumb over hers. He heard her sharp intake of breath and let go. "I'll see you in two hours," he said, and noticed his voice was huskier than he'd expected.

He also noticed she didn't move from the spot when he left the room. As he walked down the hall, he shook his head. He couldn't deny being attracted to her. But he'd been attracted to women before, and, except for the few times before he knew better, the relationship hadn't become serious. There wasn't any reason to think he couldn't handle it this time. No reason at all.

Lizzie watched Hank Davis leave her office, then took a step back, grabbed the edge of her desk for support and bit back the groan that threatened to give her away. Her legs had turned to rubber the first moment she had laid eyes on him in the reception area of Images, Inc. Hunk? The word made her want to laugh out loud. What an understatement! And she had to work with this man? Every day? Possibly evenings? This time, the groan was impossible to keep inside.

With an unsteady step, she walked to the door and quietly closed it, fighting the urge to follow him down the hall for another look at him. Leaning her forehead against the smooth, cool wood, she was tempted to start banging it. She would never be able to keep her wits about her for the next two weeks if she didn't pound some sense into her foggy mind.

His voice, low and lazy, like a river slowly moving along a grassy bank on a summer day, had sent warm currents flowing through her body. But it was his dimples that had done her in. Those twin valleys bracketing a sexy mouth had made that smile a true kneeweakener. And Lizzie's knees felt like warm jelly again, just thinking about them.

She quickly scolded herself for her weakness. She didn't have time for men, no matter how good-looking. Her life was full enough with Images, Inc., and with Amanda, her daughter.

On her way to her desk, she grabbed the folder she had left on the sofa, hoping to get her mind back on business. But it was impossible. The moment he had looked up from the magazine in his hand, she knew she was in for a difficult time. Professionalism had flown out the window. Clear brown eyes had stared into hers, and she had detected a decided twinkle in them.

Determined to get herself under control, she pressed the intercom button and asked Janine to step into her office. She had a lot to do before she picked up Hank at his hotel.

Janine opened the door and poked her head into the office. "Mercy, that is some man you're going to be working with."

Lizzie smiled at her best friend and employee and prayed Janine wouldn't see how much Hank Davis had rattled her. "You gave him the folder with the schedule, didn't you?"

"Of course." Stepping into the room, Janine perched on the arm of the sofa and propped her chin in one hand, her hazel eyes dancing. "Once you're done with him, there won't be a woman within a hundred miles of Kansas City that won't be falling at his feet."

Lizzie kept her thoughts to herself. No need feeding into Janine's daydreams.

"It doesn't take much of a stretch of the imagination to see him all spiffed up in a custom-made tux and starched shirt, charming the Kansas City social set," Janine continued.

"Clothes can sometimes make the man," Lizzie said without thinking. And that's what worried her. Good-looking men in tuxedos had always been her weakness. Amanda's father had been the first proof of that.

But even in something as mundane as a blue chambray shirt and jeans, Henry Wallace Davis was a sight to behold. He didn't look like the type who would be comfortable in a business suit. He was too rugged, too rough around the edges. And it was now her job to smooth out those edges.

"Mr. Davis seems pretty well made to me," Janine said with another sigh. "But you'll know how to handle him."

Just the thought of "handling" Hank Davis sent a shiver through Lizzie. She shoved the thought from her mind and returned to the business at hand. "Would you call Bailey and tell him to have the car here in about an hour? I need to return Mrs. Adams's call at the convalescent center about my mom."

"How's she doing?"

"Better. The nurses think the doctor will let her come home soon. That will be a big relief."

"And more work for you," Janine pointed out.

"I'll deal with it." She placed a finger on her temple, massaging the headache threatening her clear thinking. "I have to. Even with the fee from Hank Davis, we need to bring in more clients. There's no getting around that. We both know business has been slow this spring. Do you have any idea who called earlier?"

Janine shook her head. "He asked for you and I told him you were with a client. Before I could ask for a name, he'd hung up."

"Maybe he'll call back." Lizzie didn't want to lose a chance at new business. "If he does—if you recognize his voice—put him right through."

While Janine went to make arrangements for transportation, Lizzie dialed the phone, then waited for one of the nurses to check her mother's chart. Mentally clicking off her list of things to do, she almost wished she could do without Hank Davis and his fee. But she couldn't back out because of a foolish attraction to a client. This one was too important. His deposit alone was the last step toward making the final payment on her small-business loan. Once it was paid, Images, Inc., would be free and clear. With the bank, anyway. Her mother's care and the worry over the medical bills would be a thing of the past. If they could bring in more clients, she could afford to hire more consultants, and then she would have more time to spend with Amanda.

Maybe someday she would realize her dream of making her firm the most sought after in Kansas City. If she could do that, she might prove to her family that she wasn't the wild child she once was.

One step at a time, she reminded herself.

In her heart, her daughter and family came first. She wouldn't let a man change that, and since she reluctantly admitted she was attracted to Hank, she needed to focus on his roaming life. That should keep her hormones in line. She knew his type. The moment Amanda's father had heard the word "baby," he'd hit the road and never looked back. He wasn't the only one who had left her, either. She knew, firsthand, that some men weren't the type to settle down, and she wasn't going to let herself get caught up with someone like that again. In fact, she had proven she didn't need any man, so even if Hank was stable, she still had no business letting her weak knees and her racing heart get the better of her. She had a dream and something to prove.

"What's this?" Hank asked when he stepped out of the hotel. It was obvious that the limousine parked at the curb and the uniformed driver waiting at the open door were for him.

"It's something special we do for our clients." Lizzie gave the driver a warm smile as she got into the car and motioned for Hank to follow.

He climbed in after her and settled onto the wide seat across from her. "But a limo? Isn't that kind of extravagant? I'm taking the foreman's job, not the company president's."

"It all has to do with self-image," she explained, her face intent. "If a person believes he's worthy of something, he'll live up to it eventually. A limo is something that, in most people's minds, represents a certain social and economic level. Being chauffeured in a limousine gives a person a special feeling and, in time, it begins to show in the way that person thinks of himself and acts."

"Not to mention being seen in one, right?"

She leveled her gaze on him and shot him a perfect smile. "Right."

He held her gaze, lost in the blue of her eyes until she finally looked away to give the driver instructions. Turning back to Hank when she was finished, she smiled. "Bailey will be your driver for the next two weeks. And if you need anything, let him know."

The driver smoothly pulled the limo out of the parking lot and into the steady stream of traffic. "Call me any time, Mr. Davis."

"Thanks." Stretching out his legs in the roomy interior, Hank accidentally nudged Lizzie's foot, only to see her shift away from him. "And the name's Hank."

"Yessir."

Hank glanced at the woman across from him as the glass went up, cutting them off from Bailey. With nothing else to do, he'd spent the two hours since he'd left her office doing little more than thinking about her. Dressed in the same creamy-white suit, with her deep red hair still neatly bundled up on the back of her head, she looked glossy and crisp, exactly like the ad for her company. Professional. Untouchable. But Hank had an idea that she used her own psychology on herself. Things were not always what they seemed. Just like the limo.

Shifting in his seat, he caught her attention. "While I was reading through the contract, I had a question."

"What's that?" she asked and leaned forward.

The scent of her perfume, sweet yet musky, drifted in Hank's direction, taking his concentration to continue. "You mentioned that you usually work at least a month with the people who hire you. Since I only have two weeks, maybe I should just be paying for a half course."

Her eyes widened, and the pulse beating at the base of her throat picked up speed. "We'll just double our efforts," she said, her voice slightly unsteady.

Her answer narrowed down the possibilities that

had run through his mind while he had waited for her to arrive. She needed the money. Luckily he didn't. He'd made good money at every job he'd ever worked, and there had been no expenses but his own day-to-day living. The foreman's job would pay better than he'd been getting on his old crew, so he didn't have to worry. But he wondered why, with a fancy business, money was an issue for her.

"Where's our first stop?" he asked.

She cleared her throat and tugged at the hem of her skirt. "The apartment won't be ready until tomorrow, so I thought we'd start with some shopping at The Plaza today."

"Shopping?"

"Clothes shopping."

He wasn't surprised. She obviously believed the outside was the place to start. "Clothes make the man, huh?" he asked with a grin.

She lifted her head and stared at him. "How did you—" A blush painted her cheekbones and she pressed her lips together.

"How did I know? Well, the limo is as much for show as for the self-image," he explained, enchanted by her high color. "Clothes would be the same."

"You're much more perceptive than I'd imagined. Do you have it all figured out?"

Her smile was sincere, and he knew she'd just paid him a compliment. "Not all of it. Is this what you do for fun?"

"Fun?" She shook her head. "I don't have much time for fun. Running a business takes a lot of time."

"But everybody should take the time to cut loose and have some fun once in a while."

"I agree, but it depends on your definition of the word," she pointed out.

Hank thought about it. For most of his life, he had done what he wanted, when he wanted. Life had been hard at times, but he had never failed to enjoy it. So why had he signed up to have his "image" changed?

Because he'd been bored. Because the ad in the magazine had caught his attention, and he thought it might be fun. And it wouldn't hurt to make a good impression. He'd still be Hank, when all was said and done. New clothes wouldn't change that.

He shot her his best grin. "I think working with you is going to be fun. What do you think?"

She opened her mouth to answer, then shut it again. "I think it'll be interesting."

For the time being, her answer was good enough for him, but it definitely raised his curiosity.

Chapter Two

"But I like blue jeans."

Hank's announcement brought stares from the other customers in the expensive men's clothing store, and he nearly laughed. He didn't give a fig what he wore. Never had. But he wanted to put a little scratch in the veneer Lizzie wore and see her reaction.

Holding a pair of khaki trousers draped over one arm, her face was a mask of patience and calm. "There are times and places for denim, Hank. Trust me. But you'll need something for your first day at Crown and something for casual wear."

"That's what jeans are for," he argued, while she nudged him toward the dressing room. It was on the tip of his tongue to tell her she could wear the damned pants herself, when her features softened, and he saw her bite back a smile.

So, she does know how to loosen up. She just didn't want to do it. He would remember that. Maybe the next two weeks wouldn't be so bad, after all.

"We'll check out the jeans as soon as we've finished with these." With another nudge in the direction of the dressing room, she handed him the khakis. "Please, Hank?"

Whether it was the tone of her voice or the sound of his name, he didn't know. He stopped in his tracks and took the pants from her. "Now, how can I say no when I can see how much it means to you?"

Her grateful smile was enhanced by the shades of rose blooming on her cheeks. She pulled another item from a rack. "And take this shirt with you," she said, pressing a sport shirt into his free hand. "Oh, and these pants and shirt, too."

Hank chuckled and shook his head. "Do all your clients get this kind of special treatment?"

"Of course they do. All my clients are special." She turned around and headed in the direction of one of the clerks.

In the dressing room, he was ready to dump the pile on the floor and tell her everything fit fine, but he thought better of the idea. She had a point. He wanted to look his best for the new job. It was important that he make a good impression. Whether he stuck with the job or not, he wanted to start out on the right foot. Wasn't that why he'd hired Lizzie?

He stripped out of the clothes he felt most comfortable in—had always felt most comfortable in— and into the clothes she'd given him.

He didn't bother with the mirror when he stepped out of the dressing room. Instead he went looking for Lizzie and found her comparing ties. "How's this?" he asked, standing beside her.

"Oh, Hank, they're perfect!"

The admiring gleam in her eye and the smile on

her face took him by surprise. He shrugged to cover it and tried for indifference. "If you like it, it's good enough for me. I hate to admit it, Lizzie, but you have good taste. I only have one question."

She looked up from the tie she was holding against a shirt. "What's that?"

"Are you helping me pick out my underwear, too?" he asked, giving in to the temptation to tease her.

"Hank!"

Her eyes, wide with surprise, closed, and she pursed her lips. Then he saw her bite back a smile and noticed how her shoulders shook. He'd hit his mark. "Come on. Socks and shorts are over here," he said taking her arm and propelling her to the other side of the store.

"Stop, Hank!" she cried, laughing.

Her words didn't stop him, but the sound of her bubbling laughter did. It was like flowers bursting open in the springtime. Warm and refreshing. He looked at her and saw a sparkle and shine in her eyes that made his heart skip a beat. That wasn't good. He needed to get a grip. Fun was fun, but... He wasn't in the habit of falling too hard for women, but just because it hadn't happened before, didn't mean it wouldn't. Considering the circumstances, this was the wrong woman to be the first.

She was the first to regain her composure. "I—I think I'll leave those to you, if that's all right."

"Yeah," he said, still stunned. "I think I can handle it myself."

She slipped from his grasp and took a few steps away from him, then turned back. "When you're finished, we'll take care of the purchases."

He started for the dressing room, only to see his reflection in the mirror, surprised that he looked like the same old Hank, only...different. Behind him, Lizzie stood watching. Their gazes met, and once again his heart skipped. Damn!

Before he had a chance to think of something to say to lighten the moment, she spun on her heel and found the nearest clerk. "We'll take what we've already chosen and everything in the dressing room," he heard her say.

The clerk glanced from her to Hank, then hesitated before ringing up the assortment of items. Letting out the breath he hadn't realized he'd been holding, Hank returned to the dressing room and quickly changed back into his familiar jeans and shirt.

When he had finished, he met Lizzie at the counter and gave the purchases to the clerk. While the young man tallied their total, Hank reached for the pen Lizzie held poised to sign the receipt and slipped it from her fingers.

"What are you doing?" she asked.

"They're my clothes, I'll pay for them."

"It's part of the agreement," she replied and attempted to retrieve the pen.

"I'm taking care of it anyway." He placed the pen on the counter far enough away so Lizzie couldn't reach it. Digging in his back pocket, he pulled out his wallet and slipped out his credit card.

"Hank—"

"Don't worry about it. I've got it covered. If we're going to argue about every penny, then you'll have to find another guy."

Pearly teeth scraped her lower lip, her eyes narrowed and frown lines appeared between them. "All right," she relented. "This time. But really, Hank—"

He gave her a look that silenced her, then signed the receipt the clerk slid across the counter. "There," he said, grabbing the bags in one hand and taking her arm with the other. "That's all settled. Now we can get those jeans."

Lizzie glanced at her watch. "We'll have to do it tomorrow. You have a date at the fitness center."

"Fitness center? You're kidding."

She swept past him to the door. "You'll need to keep fit," she said as she stepped outside. "And the gym is the perfect place to meet people. You're new in town. You'll want to make some friends you can—"

"Hang out with?" he finished for her.

"Exactly."

He caught up with her on the sidewalk and Bailey took the packages from him. "Wait just a minute, Lizzie. I've played a little pickup basketball in my life and lifted some barbells, but I doubt I've ever stepped foot in the kind of place you're talking about. I'll be a real fish out of water."

She slid him a glance he couldn't read, then slipped into the open door of the limo. He followed her, but couldn't help glancing at the curve of her thigh as he settled across from her. It was getting to be a bad habit. One that needed breaking as soon as possible. Lizzie was far too tempting for his peace of mind. If this kept up, he wouldn't last two weeks.

They rode a few blocks in silence before she spoke again. "You need to understand that being a member of this particular center is important," she said, stubbornly refusing to budge on the subject. "Your membership at the fitness center and at other places throughout the city are key to becoming a part of the Kansas City business world. Even more importantly, it gets you into the heart of Kansas City society."

"Kansas City society doesn't interest me, and I'm taking the foreman's job, not CEO's. I'm a simple guy, Lizzie. I want to improve myself, but not that much. That's not where I'm headed." Besides, the idea of a gym was to help a person get fit. He was fit. He didn't need any of those newfangled machines to keep him that way. Hard, physical labor was what kept a man in top condition. And he told her so.

"Not everyone has the opportunity to do that kind of work. Most successful businessmen spend the majority of their time behind a desk. I'm sure you'll find that a visit to the center several times a week will be a big help."

He considered it. True, his job wouldn't be physical, like the work he had done for most of his life. He would spend most of his time behind a desk dealing with subcontractors and suppliers and only overseeing the work on the site. The lack of physical labor could have a bad effect on him. But just the thought of working out in a gym left him cold.

"Do you go to a gym?" he asked.

"Not this particular one. But, yes, I do visit a fitness center at least once a week. And I try to run or walk when I can."

Hank shook his head and grinned. "All that and assisting me. Where will you find the time?"

She gave him a stern look. "I'll find the time to work out. I like to stay in shape."

He made himself comfortable and looked her up

and down. "I'd say you've managed to do that. Very well. Now, about that gym..."

She leaned forward, her frown marring her pretty features. "You agreed to put yourself in my hands. You paid good money to hire me. Why don't you let me do my job?"

He had a feeling he was going to be trying her patience to the extreme. But she was right. He had hired her to do a job. He might as well let her do it and get his money's worth. "Tell you what. I'll go to this gym on one condition."

She leaned back in the seat again, hesitancy and a glimmer of distrust in her eyes. "And what might that be?"

He was ready to bounce the ball in her court to see how far she was willing to go to do her job. "I'll climb on every last one of those machines, I'll even have one of those massages if they give them there, but I want you right beside me. Is it a deal?"

"I... Hank, that isn't fair. I'm not accustomed to some of the exercise equipment."

"And I've never used any of it." He let a slow smile spread over his face. "It's the only way you're going to get me in the door," he challenged her.

She turned to gaze out the window, and he could almost hear the wheels in her mind churning. Just when he thought he'd won, she turned back, her eyes bright and her smile wicked. "I don't have my exercise clothes with me."

This time, his smile was sincere. "I don't have any, either."

"We'll buy them—" Her mouth snapped shut.

Hank crossed his arms on his chest, leaned back against the plush leather of the interior of the limo and chuckled. Now that the notion to share the experience with her had struck, he liked the idea of seeing her in a set of exercise clothes. "I think my bank account can accommodate some for you, too."

Lizzie instantly forgot about how uncomfortable she was in a leotard when she saw Hank in a T-shirt bearing the gym insignia and a pair of way-too-snug-for-her-sanity shorts.

She gasped, then swallowed and tried not to stare. Muscled men weren't her style, but she would have had to have been blind not to react to the sight before her. And she was far from blind.

"Okay, Lizzie, what do you want to try first?"

She blinked.

"Lizzie?"

Two more blinks, and she snapped out of the fog to look him in the eye. "Huh?"

Hank's dimples deepened to craters. "You know more about these contraptions than I do. Where do we start?"

Her knees grew rubbery and she gave herself a mental shake. Being attracted to this man would be hazardous. And very wrong. She'd already failed with men in the past, and although the first had left her with the best thing that had ever happened to her, she wouldn't make that mistake again. Nor would she repeat the second one. She quickly reminded herself that Hank was a client and nothing more than a construction worker from New Mexico who was simply stepping up into a foreman's position. He obviously wanted to better himself, but would he stick with it? Not exactly the kind of man she should be attracted to, if she had the inclination. She didn't. And she didn't have the time. She needed to keep that in perspective.

"Here comes Tony," she said, spying one of the trainers. "He can show you how to use the equipment."

After introducing the two men, she followed behind them while they made the rounds of the gym. It irked her that the sight of Tony's extremely well-toned body didn't bother her in the least, whereas just a peek at Hank's sent her heart rate zipping.

Hank climbed off the gym's latest mechanical acquisition and turned to her. "It's your turn."

She took a step back to avoid being too close to him. No reason to tempt her hormones. "Thanks, I'll pass."

Before she knew what was happening, he scooped her up in his arms. "Nope, can't do that. We have an agreement," he said, placing her on the padded bench.

And she'd thought her heart was racing just watching him! Her skin burned where he gripped her calf to move it into position and slip her foot into the stirrup. She meant to protest, but her voice had deserted her. All she could do was make certain she was still breathing. That wasn't nearly as simple as it should have been.

"Hold these," he said, pressing a pair of grips in her hand. "Now, pull and glide."

Without thinking, she did as he instructed. The effort took all her concentration, and she forgot Hank was near. She'd never used the exercise equipment before. Her method of keeping her body toned consisted of a weekly aerobics class and walking whenever possible. But the machine wasn't bad. In fact, she found it almost enjoyable.

A hand touched her shoulder.

"Unless you're used to this, you'd better stop."

She looked up into Hank's eyes and lost her bearings. When his hand remained in place for a moment too long, she shifted her position. "You're right. I'll pay for this tomorrow."

His shrug sent his muscles rippling beneath his shirt. "You'll be fine."

Lizzie could only nod. He reached out a hand to assist her, and she took it. Big mistake. Her gaze met his, and it was as if her soul were exposed to him in full view.

She reclaimed her hand as gently as possible. "Thanks," she murmured.

Tony interrupted them to ask Hank a question, giving her a brief reprieve and the chance to pull herself together. She escaped to the fruit bar where she ordered a bottle of water, then turned and leaned back to watch Hank and Tony.

A small crowd had gathered around the machine where Hank worked out. Lizzie occasionally glimpsed him through the bodies blocking her view. Those brief peeks were more than enough for her, and she silently sent up thanks that she couldn't see more.

Hank didn't resemble Mr. Universe. His physique wasn't that extreme. But the thought of professional bodybuilders still flashed through her mind while she watched. Sweat darkened the fabric of his T-shirt and glistened on his skin. Biceps bulged and strained. She could hear his slightly labored breathing and soft grunts of exertion. His dark hair, too long to suit her usual tastes, stuck to his neck in individual curls. And that was only the top half of him.

She dared to lower her gaze to his legs. Powerful thighs bunched and stretched as he raised and lowered himself. Men's legs had always fascinated her. Hank's mesmerized her.

The sound of counting reached her ears. "One hundred fifty-three, one hundred fifty-four, one hundred fifty..."

Holy cow! She tore her gaze away and slammed the water bottle on the bar. Enough. Without another look, she retreated to the dressing room and changed back into her suit, all the while berating herself for her weakness. She'd make sure to keep her distance and not put herself in a position like this again. Any attraction to the man would be disastrous, and she'd almost gone way beyond that. She had her business to think about. And Amanda. Her daughter had been hurt once because of an attraction to a man. She wouldn't let that happen again.

Lizzie wanted so badly to give Amanda the best. She had done all she could, but so much of her money went to daycare for Amanda and the rest had gone to pay most of her mother's medical bills. The stroke her mother had suffered had been severely debilitating, but her mother had worked hard for months in the rehab center to regain much of what she had lost.

Since her husband's death, three years earlier, Lizzie's mother had relied on family. Even more on Lizzie than she had on Lizzie's sister, who was six years older. At thirty, Vicky had her own family and the perfect life, as she'd always had. With the added expense of their brother's college fees, they'd struggled. But even more, Lizzie wanted to be a success, not a failure. Her parents had tried to curb her wild streak, but she hadn't listened to them. She understood now that it was simply her way to gain attention. Her sister, Vicky, had just married the perfect man and was planning the perfect family and life. Lizzie had always been the younger and less perfect daughter. She had come home from college to announce that she was pregnant and the father had left her high and dry. She had broken her parents' hearts and, even though their disappointment and disapproval had been evident, they had stood by her. She'd learned her lesson the hard way. Her father had died before she could prove to him that she had changed, but she could still show her mother that she was a responsible woman and mother.

"Giving up?"

Lizzie jerked her thoughts from the past and looked up to see Hank standing in front of her, a white towel draped around his neck. "It's a little more than I'm used to," she told him with a smile she didn't feel.

"Hungry?"

She nodded. "A little." In fact, she realized she hadn't eaten a thing since breakfast.

"Good," he said, his dimples deepening. "Bailey told me about a great place to eat. I'll have a quick shower in the locker room and we can—"

"Hank," she said, reaching out to lay a hand on his muscled forearm. A shiver of heat ran up her arm, but she ignored it. "We can't have dinner tonight."

He turned to her, his expression one of confusion. "Why not? I thought it would be the perfect chance for you to tell me which fork to use and how I'm not supposed to tuck the napkin under my chin."

She wasn't sure if she should tell him the truth.

She rarely told men about her daughter. Another hard lesson learned, and at Amanda's expense. And she never revealed her private life to clients. But for some reason she knew she had to tell Hank.

"I promised my daughter I would have dinner with her tonight."

For a moment, he was silent. "Your daughter?"

Lizzie recognized his disappointment, so like the other men she'd known in the past. She knew better. Even worse, she was disappointed. It shouldn't have bothered her, but it did.

"A daughter," Hank repeated, feeling as if he had been sucker punched. He had never asked for any particulars about Lizzie's family, but he hadn't thought it was important. Apparently it was, even though he wanted to deny it.

With a quick—and he hoped discreet—glance at her left hand, he assured himself that she wasn't wearing a ring. He hadn't noticed one before, but he hadn't paid much attention and didn't trust his memory.

"I'm sorry about dinner," she said.

He shook his head. "No, it's okay."

She lifted her gaze to his and he saw a touch of sadness in her blue eyes. Because they couldn't have dinner? He had no way of knowing.

It didn't matter. Things were now changed. Lizzie was no longer simply a beautiful woman he was attracted to. She was a mother. A woman with the responsibility of a child. A family. Something he had only vague memories of and no plans to have for his own.

But his curiosity was getting the better of him, even

though he now saw her in a new and very different light. "How old is she? Your...daughter."

"Four." She glanced around the crowded gym as if she were looking for the way out. "Maybe we should leave."

Nodding, he slipped the towel from his neck. "I'll grab that shower and meet you at the car. Unless you want to wait for me here?"

She shook her head. "I'll go on and let Bailey know you'll be out soon."

All he could do was nod again and head for the showers. The fact that she was a mother didn't make her less attractive. It made her more attractive because of his curiosity. But if she was married— No, he was certain she wasn't. She would wear a ring. Wouldn't she?

It took him less than fifteen minutes to shower and change, then he met Lizzie in front of the building, where Bailey waited with the limo. Still wondering how to handle the change in circumstances, he climbed in to take the seat across from her. Bailey slid behind the wheel and the car merged into the traffic.

"We have a full day scheduled tomorrow," Lizzie said without looking at him. "The apartment is furnished and will be ready to move into. I'll explain the details later so you don't need to worry. You'll be able to move in first thing in the morning. Do you have your belongings stored somewhere, or do you plan to send for them?"

Thinking of his meager collection of belongings stowed in the dilapidated pull-behind trailer he'd lived in for years, he couldn't think of a single thing he hadn't brought with him that would suit a subleased apartment. "I won't be needing anything."

"I'll let Bailey know we need to pick you up around eight in the morning."

Checking his watch, he realized it was earlier than he thought. So what was he supposed to do with himself for the rest of the evening? He hadn't made any plans.

"I thought we were on some kind of accelerated schedule," he reminded her.

"We are," she agreed, "but I always spend at least one evening a week with my daughter, whenever possible.

He was hesitant to ask the next question, but he had to know the answer. "I understand, but what about her father? Couldn't he take her, considering our schedule?"

She was silent for a moment. "She doesn't have a father," she said in a voice so soft he nearly missed it.

Hank let her remark sink in before asking the next obvious question. "Does that mean you don't have a husband lurking in the shadows, ready to clobber me if I step out of line?"

"No, no husband."

Her direct gaze spoke volumes. She was a single woman. A single *mother*. Even though his memories of his own mother had faded with time, he had an idea of what it took to be a mother. Time. Lots of time. And money. He suspected that wasn't something Lizzie had an abundance of, in spite of appearances.

"You said you have family here in Kansas City,"

he said, steering the conversation in a different direction.

Startled, she turned to look at him. "Why, yes. There's my mother, my sister and brother."

"Older or younger?"

She folded her hands neatly in her lap. "My sister is six years older, married, with two children. My brother is attending college."

"Sounds like a nice family."

"It is," she answered with a soft, loving smile that struck his heart. But her smile vanished. "I—I wasn't the easiest daughter to raise."

He saw pain clearly reflected in her eyes and heard the sorrow in her voice. It was another view of her that caused him to wonder why. "It happens to a lot of people," was all he could say.

They rode a few blocks, both lost in their own thoughts, and an idea began to form in Hank's mind. He really didn't want to spend an entire evening alone in his hotel room, and he wasn't in the mood to sightsee. "Where are you and your daughter having dinner? Maybe you could both teach me which fork to use."

Lizzie's laughter was so soft, he barely caught it. "The last time I checked with Emily Post, pizza is eaten with the fingers."

"Pizza? Hey, I love pizza! But some people do eat it with a knife and fork."

Eyes narrowing, she cocked her head to one side and looked at him. "Are you by any chance hinting at an invitation?"

He knew he should be ashamed or even a little embarrassed. He wasn't. "So can I come along?"

Her laughter rang out clear and loud in the padded

and plush interior of the limousine. "I doubt you'd want to spend an evening eating pizza with a four-year-old. There are times she would try the patience of a saint, even though she's usually an angel."

He didn't doubt that for a minute, not with Lizzie for a mother. And he didn't know why he felt this need to join them, other than not wanting to spend the evening alone, staring at a television screen in his hotel room. He had often spent evenings watching TV in his trailer. It wasn't something as simple as nervous energy, either. He'd spent that in the gym. No, it had to be curiosity. What kind of woman really existed beyond what the eye saw? What was her story? He had heard all kinds, so nothing would surprise him. And what kind of mother was she? He hadn't expected this added twist. And although it ought to put him off, it made everything even more intriguing.

"Kids don't bother me," he said with a shrug. It was true, because he didn't really know kids. He'd never wanted to be a family man, so he hadn't been around them much. But he was willing to do it, for the sake of curiosity and to spend a little time with Lizzie.

"I don't know..."

It was better than a refusal, and her hesitancy gave him the courage to push. "You can explain the sublease to me tonight and save some time tomorrow. I'll even spring for the pizza."

"I can't let you do that."

"Then we'll go Dutch," he pushed on.

"Well..."

"Good, it's settled." He turned and rapped on the tinted glass separating them from Bailey. When the glass came down, he gave the driver instructions.

"Drop me off at my hotel, then take Miss Edwards to her home and wait. When she and her daughter are ready to leave, pick them up, and then come by the hotel for me."

"Yessir."

Before Hank could remind him that he wasn't a "sir," Bailey had raised the window again. Pleased that Lizzie hadn't interrupted with excuses, Hank leaned back in his seat and studied her. He had to admit she didn't look all that happy about being railroaded, but she didn't look like she'd go off like a cannon, either. In fact, she looked more astounded than anything. Fine with him. Whatever it took. Even if it meant spending an evening with a four-year-old.

Chapter Three

"Are you my mommy's cwient?" Amanda asked, her mouth surrounded by tomato sauce. Lizzie knew it wouldn't do any good to try to clean her daughter's face until the pizza was gone or her child had had enough to eat. In thirty seconds, the angelic mouth would bear another red ring.

Hank swallowed the bite he'd just taken and smiled at Amanda. "I sure am. Her friend, too, I hope." Directing his gaze at Lizzie, his dimples deepened.

Lizzie tried to shield herself from reacting to his smile, but she hadn't found a way yet. He had more charm than any man should. Unfortunately his charm tended to turn her knees to the consistency of pudding.

"Are you my fwiend, too?" Amanda asked.

And didn't it figure that he was winning her daughter over with the same charm? If he could bottle it, he'd make a fortune.

"Only if that's okay with you," Hank answered

with a note of sincerity Lizzie couldn't help but believe.

She watched as he stuck out his hand and wondered if her daughter would remember what the gesture required. If she did, Hank was a brave man, considering the smear of grease, tomato sauce and cheese covering Amanda's miniature hand.

Amanda hesitated for a moment, studying Hank's offer, then placed her hand in his. "Sure. We can be fwiends."

Hank didn't even flinch at the gooey mess he encountered. Instead he gave Amanda one good shake, but didn't let go. "You know, Amanda, you're even prettier than your mommy. Smart, too, I'll bet."

"I know my affabet," she said, her face serious.

"Really? Then you are smart. So what do you do for fun?"

Lizzie smothered the groan that threatened. Fun seemed to be Hank's favorite pastime.

Her face scrunched in puzzlement, Amanda turned to Lizzie, then back to Hank. "Well... I visit my gwamma and sometimes I get to play wif Denny and Woger, but they're boys, so they get mean."

"Denny and Roger are my sister's boys. Amanda stays with her when I have to work in the evening," Lizzie explained. "They're a little older and sometimes get carried away."

Hank's eyebrows knitted in what was obviously concern when he looked at Amanda. "Do they hurt you?"

She shook her head, sending her carroty curls dancing. "No, but they make me mad and I cwy sometimes."

"Maybe I should teach you a few—"

"Hank," Lizzie interrupted, placing her hand on his arm. The warmth that shot through her made her pause for a moment to catch her breath. Hoping he hadn't noticed her reaction, she did her best to ignore it and continued. "Hank, believe me, Amanda takes care of herself. Sometimes they torment her a little, but they adore her."

Instead of relieving his worry, his frown deepened. "They shouldn't do that. Torment her, I mean. But it's easy to see why they adore her." His frown instantly turned to a smile when he looked at Amanda.

Lizzie felt her heart warm toward him, which was the last thing she wanted. Most men, when they met her daughter, talked to her from an adult level. But something about Hank and the way he related to Amanda was different. And a bit scary, considering how much she, herself, was attracted to him.

"You were an only child, right? She can hold her own," Lizzie replied, knowing she could use a few pointers on how to protect herself from Hank's charm.

"Can her mother?" he asked.

His gaze met hers and she nearly melted into a puddle. There was no way she could answer, and when she started to pull her hand away, he covered it with his, trapping her. It felt so comforting, she couldn't do anything more than sit staring into his eyes.

"I need a nakkin," Amanda announced.

It took a supreme effort for Lizzie to drag her gaze and her hand from Hank's. "I'll get some, sweetie," she said in a shaky voice and rose from her chair.

"Mind if I have another piece of that pizza?" she heard Hank ask her daughter.

Lizzie missed Amanda's answer as she retrieved

several napkins from an empty booth. She was glad for the interruption. She'd expected her daughter to be a solid distraction from Hank's charisma, but instead, Amanda seemed to draw out more of his charm. Lizzie chided herself for being glad he had joined them. She shouldn't be. It wasn't right, no matter how much his hand on hers had made it feel like it was. She had been through this once before and had vowed, while dealing with Amanda's tears, never to repeat the mistake.

Hank is a client, she reminded herself. Probably not a man with much staying power, if his past was any indication. And it always was. If she'd learned one thing in her business, it was that she might be able to change a few things about people, but their general disposition and character remained static.

But maybe... No. Learning to pick the right clothes and knowing the correct thing to say in a given situation was one thing. But turning someone from a person who never settled in one place for long to a homebody wasn't possible. She needed to remember that whenever Hank's dimples scrambled her senses.

Feeling only a little better, Lizzie approached the table and heard Hank telling Amanda about the pony he had once owned when he was a boy.

Amanda's elbows were propped on the table, her face cupped in her sticky hands, as she stared at him in awe. "Did he pwance like the ponies in the circus? I wuv them! They have pwetty feathers on their heads."

"No, but he could run like the wind," he answered.

The wistful look on his face nearly undid Lizzie, and she had to stop herself from reaching out to give him a comforting hug. What was she thinking? She needed to keep her distance, both physically and emotionally, from this man.

Instead of giving in to her urge, she approached her daughter. "Let's get you cleaned up a little, then we'd better head home."

"Alweady?" Amanda asked, clearly disappointed that her mother would bring an end to her enchanted evening.

Lizzie wiped her daughter's hands and face as best she could, and Amanda didn't protest. It was one thing Lizzie had always been proud of in her daughter. Amanda knew better than to argue when told it was time for the fun to be over. Denny and Roger weren't always so easy.

As she worked to gather the mess, Hank left the table, headed in the direction of the cash register. "Where do you think you're going?" Lizzie called out to him.

"Just taking care of the tab," he answered over his shoulder without stopping.

She dropped the wad of napkins and hurried after him. "We agreed this would be Dutch treat."

"I changed my mind," he said with a shrug and kept walking.

Grabbing his arm in hopes of bringing him to a halt, a vision of him pumping iron at the gym popped into her mind, and she had to force herself to breathe. "You can't."

He slowed, but he didn't stop. "No big deal."

"It is to me." When he came to a halt and turned to look at her, she let go of him and did her best to hold her ground. "I can't let you go on paying for things, Hank. You haven't even started your new job yet."

"I invited myself along. I know that's a little on the rude side, but I'm glad I did. You saved me from spending a boring night in my hotel room. Why not let me make it up to you by paying for the pizza? It isn't like twenty bucks is going to bankrupt me."

The reminder of where she would be if she lost Hank as a client struck home. Besides, she needed to watch her pennies, in spite of the hefty chunk he had already paid to Images, Inc. But to let him pay for their evening out was another thing.

Hank leaned close and whispered, "Next time it's your treat, I promise."

The sound of his deep voice skipped over every nerve in her body, even though she knew she shouldn't let it happen. How many times in her life had men made her feel this wonderful? Only two that she could recall, and neither had affected her with the potency Hank did now. But one had led to trouble... and Amanda. The other had caused heartbreak for a two-year-old. She wouldn't let it happen again. She couldn't.

She took a step back, out of his range. "I'll hold you to that."

He tossed her another one of his winning smiles. While he was busy paying their bill, Lizzie went back to the table and finished cleaning the mess, both on the table and on her daughter.

"Is Hank coming home wif us, Mommy?"

Lizzie jerked her head up, rendered speechless by her daughter's question, and stared at her. Amanda didn't take to men. Not since Ken had broken her heart. And here she was, asking if Hank was coming home with them. Lizzie was in trouble.

"Hank is going back to his hotel room."

"Is that where his family is?"

Lizzie swallowed the lump that had suddenly formed in her throat. "N-no. Hank doesn't have any family, sweetie."

"He doesn't?" She tugged on her mother's sleeve. "Can we take him home wif us then?"

Sighing, Lizzie shook her head. "Amanda, you can't bring home stray people like you do stray kitties," she tried to explain. "But it's very nice of you to think of him. He'll be fine at the hotel tonight, and then I'll take him to his new apartment tomorrow. Does that help?"

Amanda's lower lip quivered and her eyes filled with tears. "I guess so," she said in a sad whisper.

Lizzie gave her daughter a hug, her heart filled with pride at Amanda's caring generosity, but she knew she needed to be cautious. "All ready?" she asked, when Hank returned.

"You bet." He helped Amanda down from her seat and held her hand as they walked to the exit. With her other, she grabbed Lizzie's hand. *Just like a family.* Lizzie shook the thought from her mind to focus on her daughter's chatter about her cousins' new rabbit, the neighbor's new kittens, and how she would have a zoo when she was bigger. Hank's attention was riveted on the child, and Lizzie wasn't sure what to do about this new situation. When Amanda made someone a friend, it was forever. Hank would only be a client for a few weeks, and after that there would be no reason for Lizzie to see him again. She could accept that. But could Amanda say goodbye to him when the time came? And did Lizzie really want her to?

* * *

Hank watched Lizzie fit the key into the lock of the apartment he would be trying on for size. She had explained to him earlier that after the month was over, he would decide if he wanted to continue to live there under a sublease, or whether he would find another apartment. As far as he was concerned, it didn't matter one bit where he lived, as long as he had a roof over his head and a bed to sleep in. He had spent most of his life in some sort of portable home, or at least a temporary one. None had been much to brag about. In fact, he couldn't remember the last time he'd been in a place as nice as his hotel room.

The door swung open and Lizzie glanced over her shoulder at him while he waited quietly behind her. Her face was blank, except for a tiny crease between her eyes.

She was back to being Elizabeth Edwards, Images, Inc., owner. He frowned at the thought. She had been relaxed the night before. In fact, he felt he could honestly say they had had fun. What had happened to make her change overnight?

With a professional smile pasted on her face, she stepped into the dim silence of the apartment. "Well, here we are. I hope you'll find everything to your liking, but if there's anything you need, just let me know."

He moved into the entryway behind her and stood peering into the room ahead. He couldn't see much, but what he did left him speechless. He could've put his trailer and a couple of others just like it into the room and still had space for more.

"Once you've added your own personal things, it'll seem more like home," she continued as she flipped on a set of low lights and walked into the living room.

Following her, he looked around and thought of the few things he had brought with him on his flight. There weren't many. Enough to fit in a suitcase, along with his clothes. Even if he'd brought everything he had left behind in his trailer back in Albuquerque, it wouldn't make a difference. This was a whole new world to him.

"Nice place," he finally said.

Her false smile eased and she looked more like the Lizzie from the night before. "I'm glad you like it. I'll show you the rest of the apartment."

Motioning for him to follow, she led him through the living room, pointing out where the remote control for the television and the thermostat were. "Those seem to be the two most important items to most men," she said with a soft laugh. "Those and the kitchen."

When Hank didn't comment, she led him through the rest of the apartment, consisting of a small dining area off the kitchen, complete with a glass-topped table for two, and the kitchen itself, which he guessed would be called an "efficiency."

"The bedroom is this way," she said, and walked down a short hallway where she stopped at the door on the right and opened it. Moving aside, she let him pass by her into the room. "The bathroom is across the hall, and there's a well-stocked linen closet."

The room was much more than he had expected. Probably more than he deserved. But there was no reason he couldn't enjoy it for a while. Nodding, he turned to her. "You said we have some things to discuss?"

"Yes, we do."

In the living room again, Lizzie settled on one of

the chairs, while Hank sat across from her on a matching bronze leather sofa. She took a long drink of the iced tea she'd fixed for them from the supply of food still in the kitchen. "You have the rest of the morning to move in, but if you need more time, let me know. This afternoon, I'll give you a quick tour of the city."

"What about tonight?" he asked.

She placed her glass on the shiny surface of the table in front of her and smiled at him. "I made reservations for us at one of the most popular restaurants on The Plaza. I think you'll like it."

Hank knew he'd like any place, especially with Lizzie for company. But not if she didn't loosen up and be the Lizzie he'd shared pizza with the night before. Since she'd arrived in the limo at his hotel to pick him up for their trip to the apartment, she'd been Miss Professional, the same as she had been when he'd first met her at Images, Inc. And he had thought they were beyond that. He thought they were friends. Apparently it had only been temporary.

"One step back and two forward," he muttered.

"I'm sorry?"

"What's the name of the place?"

"The Cheesecake Factory. I think you'll enjoy it. The food is wonderful and it isn't at all formal."

"Nothing fancy for me yet, huh?" His attention was grabbed by her long legs when she moved to cross them, then she tugged at the hem of her skirt. He had noticed how she always did it whenever she was nervous.

"That's for later," she answered, her voice on the husky side. She cleared her throat and tugged on her skirt again. "We have a lot to accomplish before that.

Did you look over the information in the folder Janine gave you?"

"Some of it." That was a long stretch of the truth. He hadn't even opened it. He wasn't even sure where he had put it.

"Then let's go over the schedule now. Tomorrow, you have an appointment to get your hair cut."

"Barber shop," he said, nodding. "No big deal."

"*No-o-o-o.* A hairstylist."

"Hairstylist?" He nearly choked on the word. "Look, Lizzie, that might be the kind of thing your other clients do, but it's not for me. Construction foremen don't need to have their hair styled."

She shook her head. "It's already been taken care of." Standing, she smoothed her skirt and started for the door. "Trust me, Hank. I know what I'm doing."

"You're leaving?"

"Bailey will be back to help you move, then he'll bring me back around one, and we'll see the sights."

He stood and followed her to the door, reluctant to see her leave. "Is Amanda coming with us?"

"No, she's in preschool," she explained, then reached into her purse. "I forgot to give these to you." She handed him an envelope and he looked inside. "Everything you need should be in there. There's an extra key to the apartment, your telephone number and address with your mailbox number. Don't forget to have your mail forwarded." Reaching into her purse again, she pulled out a cell phone. "And this is for you."

He took the phone from her, his hand brushing across hers. Her sharp intake of breath was proof that she was affected by him as much as he was by her.

And he really didn't want to see her go. Not yet. "I had a real nice time last night."

"I—I enjoyed myself, too," she stuttered.

Looking down into her eyes, he was caught by the spark of fire he saw there. He placed one hand against the wall next to her, then brought his other up to touch her cheek and run his thumb across it. It brightened with crimson, and she stepped away.

"I've got to go," she said in a breathy voice. "I told Bailey I wouldn't be long, and he's probably wondering what's keeping me."

Before Hank had a chance to apologize, she was out the door and down the hallway. "One o'clock," he called to her.

When she had disappeared around the corner to the elevator, he closed the door and wondered what he should do until Bailey returned. He wandered back to the sofa where she'd sat talking to him, and he thought of Amanda. What kind of fool was he, getting involved with a single mother? He was beginning to like Lizzie too much. But there didn't seem to be anything he could do about it.

"I'll bet I have more culture than sour cream," Hank said, his face serious.

Stepping outside the door of the Nelson-Atkins Museum of Art, Lizzie pretended not to notice the twinkle in his brown eyes. They had spent the past week and a half cramming in visits to cultural exhibits and going over etiquette for any occasion Hank might encounter. She had learned that he knew more about dealing with people and situations than he gave himself credit for. And he did everything with ease, even when it was something he wasn't crazy about doing.

"Cultured sour cream?" she asked.

He grinned. "Sure. Don't you read labels?"

"Of course I do, but—" She shook her head. He had a habit of keeping her off guard. "This is the last of it," she said, returning to the subject. "We'll go back to my office, and I'll give you a list of places you can visit on your own."

"Like where?" he asked, shortening his stride to match hers.

"Places I'm sure you'll like, such as the NCAA Hall of Champions—"

"Yeah? Why have we been traipsing all over art museums and libraries when we could have been there instead?"

She hurried her steps when she spied Bailey with the limo. "Because you never would have gone to the museums and libraries on your own. This way, when someone mentions the Kemper Museum of Contemporary Art and Design, you'll know exactly what they're talking about."

They reached the car and Hank waited while Bailey opened the door for her. She settled inside, then he climbed in after her. "I have a feeling the men on the construction site won't be talking about art and design. But national collegiate basketball? Now there's a subject they'll be familiar with."

She sighed and looked him in the eye. "Did it ever occur to you that it might not hurt to know more than the men who work for you? And I'd lay odds they know quite a lot about Kansas City museums and other cultural activities, even if they've never been to any. Look at it this way, Hank, you're one up on them."

"Like knowing that Kansas City has more fountains than any city in the world except Rome? I'll be sure to bring it up when I'm arguing with subcontractors."

"It can't hurt to be educated about the area where you live," she insisted. "It's part of what I do to help people. Whatever you do with it now is up to you. After today, you're on your own."

"Right."

She wondered at his frown, which didn't include his usual mischievous look. She hated to admit that she had enjoyed the two weeks working with him. She would especially miss his stubborn reluctance to visit many of the places she had insisted on seeing, then watching his enthusiasm, once they were there. He had a way of making anything fun.

She always enjoyed her work, but Hank made it an even more enjoyable experience. Even when he argued. He was intelligent and asked questions that made her think more than she had ever needed to. Being around him meant staying on her toes. About everything. Especially the way he had of making her feel like she was someone special, without even meaning to, she was sure.

When they arrived at Images, Inc., she told Bailey to wait so he could take Hank back to his apartment. After that, Bailey wouldn't be needed again until she called for her next client.

Hank followed her into the building and down the hall to her office. "Make yourself comfortable while I talk to Janine," she told him, grabbing a folder from her desk. "I need to get some papers for you to fill out and sign, then you and I can go over what you can do on your own."

With Hank cooling his heels in her office, Lizzie

found her assistant in the reception area and asked for the required paperwork. Janine opened a drawer and pulled out some papers. "I'll have to make copies of the others. But I'm wondering something. What will you do, now that his contract is finished?"

"George Rogers said he would be ready to start after next week."

"That isn't what I meant." Janine's smile resembled the Cheshire cat's. "It's been nice seeing you with someone."

Lizzie stared at her. "I haven't 'been' with Hank. He was my client."

Janine shook her head, her grin widening. "Amanda told me about your trip to the pizza parlor. She's obviously crazy about him."

"I'll admit she took right to him," Lizzie said with some hesitancy. "But considering how he poured on the charm—"

"What about Amanda's mom?"

Feeling her face grow suddenly hot, Lizzie turned to the file cabinet and pretended to look for a file. Janine was far too perceptive for her own good. "Amanda's mom has learned to ignore the charm. It's just a part of Hank. He's that way with everyone, even the waitresses at the restaurant."

"Bet you'll miss him."

Lizzie nearly slammed her fingers in the file drawer. "I miss all my clients until a new one starts." Without saying more, she returned to her office, wondering if there was any place where she could find some safety. If it wasn't Hank assaulting her senses, it was Janine making mountains out of molehills. There was nothing going on with Hank. Nothing at all. And there wouldn't be.

Tugging at her jacket, Lizzie entered her office to find Hank sitting comfortably on the sofa and leafing through a magazine. "Janine will have the papers ready in a few minutes," she said, wondering if she could hide behind her desk. Putting as much distance—and furniture—between herself and Hank insured the barest of safety, but at least it was something.

Hank laid the magazine aside and gave her his full attention. "What do I do now?"

She suddenly wished he would be a little less easy to get along with, since their time was coming to an end. Of course, once she started listing some of the things he might want to accomplish on his own, she knew she would find resistance.

Settling in her chair where she hoped the desk would protect her, she pulled out a sheet of paper and a pen. "First, we'll see about getting you a car. You have several options. You can lease, buy, or rent. Which would you prefer?"

His brows drew together. "I suppose renting would be the most expensive, but right now, that's what would be best. I don't want to get stuck with a lease on an apartment and on a car."

She didn't miss the hint that he didn't want to make any permanent choices, which was fine with her. "We can do that later today, if you'd like. I'll make appointments for some other things that you'll need to do, too."

One dark eyebrow rose to arch over his eye. "Like what?"

She wasn't crazy about telling him that he would need to have a standing appointment at the hairstylist and might want to have a manicure. He wasn't the type to take that without an argument. A huge argument. She would simply add it to the list and let him take care of it. Or not. "Nothing for you to worry about," she said, and hurried to the next point. "You might want a few more clothes, but that's up to you, too."

"Maybe I should see what I'll need for the job," he replied, his frown deepening.

"Whatever you feel is right." If she were honest with him, he had already made some wonderful changes from the blue-jean-and-workshirt man who had walked into her office two weeks ago and she didn't expect that to change. Even today, he looked comfortable in the sport shirt and slacks they'd bought the week before on their shopping trip. Too comfortable and too good. He had been waltzing into her dreams far too often.

The door opened and Janine entered the office. "Here's the rest of the papers." She handed them to Lizzie with a sly look before leaving the room.

Lizzie quickly looked them over, then gave them to Hank. "If you'll fill them out and sign them, we'll be all finished."

Nodding, he took the pen she also offered and started reading. When he had finished, he gave them back to her. "I guess our contract has come to an end then?"

For some reason, she had trouble speaking. "Except for finding you a car."

"I can do that on my own, but thanks for the offer."

She tried for a smile, but failed. Why was she suddenly feeling sad? She was usually excited to see a client ready to go it alone. "If you need anything, feel free to contact me," she said, as she always did at the end of a contract period.

He studied her for a moment, the look in his eyes impossible to read. "I'll keep that in mind."

Knowing she needed to be at her professional best, she held out her hand. "You'll do fine, Hank."

He took her hand and flashed her a grin. "I always do. And, Lizzie?"

"Yes?" she asked, wishing he would let go of her hand so her heartbeat would return to normal.

"It's been fun."

When he had gone, she sat at her desk and took a deep breath, then let it out slowly. She was certain Hank would handle his new job with ease. He had the charm and skill to do it. And she would go on to help the next client. But she doubted anyone would affect her the way Hank had.

Chapter Four

"Daniel Wallace." Hank's new boss reached across the expansive desk to shake Hank's hand. "Good to meet you, Davis. Have a seat."

Hank took the offered hand, and almost chuckled at the irony of the situation. He hadn't known the name of the owner of Crown Construction until that moment. Daniel Wallace was not only the owner of Crown, but the owner and CEO of Wallace International, a company with its finger in more pies than Hank could count. And each pie was filled with solid gold. His own middle name was Wallace, but gold wasn't something he was familiar with.

Settling on the leather chair across the desk from the man, he waited. He was curious to know why he had gotten the letter offering him the foreman's position, but figured it didn't matter, as long as he had the job.

"Mind if I call you Henry?" Wallace asked.

"Most people call me Hank."

"Then Hank it is." Wallace rested his elbows on the desk and tented his hands in front of him. "I've always made it a practice to meet my employees and get to know them as soon as they're hired. I'll be asking a lot of personal questions, but you're free to do the same. If you feel I'm getting too personal, just say so."

"Okay." Hank was a bit taken aback by the man's unusual habit, but since he didn't have anything to hide, there wasn't any reason why he couldn't answer any question asked of him.

"I take it you aren't married, Hank."

"No. Never met a woman I felt the need to settle down with. Never felt the need to settle down, to be honest."

Wallace nodded, then leaned back in his chair, the hint of a sad smile on his face. "Since my wife's death, more years ago than I care to think about, I've enjoyed leading life on my terms, so I can understand that. Tell me a little about your family. Your father?"

"My dad was a widower for nine years until he died in an oil well accident."

"How old were you when you lost your mother?"

Wallace's eyes were bright blue and intense, and Hank reminded himself that all the Crown employees were questioned about their personal life. "I was ten."

"No brothers and sisters?"

"None. No family, that I ever knew of. Both of my parents were orphaned when they were young."

Leaning forward, Wallace glanced at a paper on his desk. "You've led an interesting life, Hank. Do you enjoy traveling?"

Hank shrugged. "I've seen and done a lot of things

most people never will. I've never known anything but traveling."

"But you managed to pick up an education."

"In bits and pieces."

"You have an associate degree in business. Do you enjoy that sort of thing?"

Hank considered the question. At the time he had started taking colleges classes during some of his slower times, he had wondered what he would ever do with what he was learning. But instead of quitting because he didn't see a future in it, he'd stuck with it, even though it had been an on-and-off thing. "It was interesting," he answered. "I enjoyed the classes and the things I learned. I never have put it to any use. Doubt if I ever will."

"Would you, if you had the chance?"

The man's eyes were even more intense than before and Hank suspected something was up. "I never gave it any thought."

"I'd like for you to think about it." Daniel Wallace stood and walked over to look out the wall of windows that presented a panoramic view of Kansas City. "We have a management position open in Crown Construction. With your degree and your firsthand knowledge of the construction business, I feel you're the man for the job." He turned around and pinned Hank with a determined glint in his eyes. "What do you say?"

Stunned, Hank didn't know how to answer. He wasn't at all sure he even wanted to try. He hadn't planned on making Kansas City his permanent home. In fact, he hadn't planned much of anything, except to work the foreman's job for a while until he felt the need to move on. He wasn't used to staying in one place for long. He'd never lived that way, even when his mom was alive.

"What makes you think I could do the job?" he asked.

For a moment, Wallace didn't speak. "You come highly recommended. You have the knowledge and the experience we're looking for."

"And if I don't like it?" Hank asked. "Or if I'm not as good at it as you seem to think I might be?"

"That isn't a problem," Wallace assured him. "We can always find a position for you. But you might want to give it a try. You have an adventurous spirit. Think of this as a new adventure."

Unsure of how to answer, Hank shook his head. "It isn't what I'm used to, that's for sure. I've never done anything like it before."

"Perhaps it's time you gave it a try."

Hank heard it as a challenge, and he had never been one to turn down a challenge. Besides, if he didn't take to it, he could always ask for the foreman's job. Or he could go back to New Mexico. His job with GJ Construction would always be there for him. Or there were other jobs he could find, if he needed one.

Standing, he approached Daniel Wallace with an outstretched hand. "Okay. I'll give it a try."

With a broad smile, Wallace shook his hand. "Good. There's some paperwork to fill out and then we'll get you started immediately. I'll show you around and introduce you to the people you'll be working with. I don't think you'll regret your decision."

Hank doubted he would. For one thing, it gave him the excuse he was looking for to see Lizzie again. He hadn't been able to get her out of his mind all weekend and had tried to think of a reason to call her, but he hadn't come up with anything. He owed Daniel Wallace a big thank-you.

"I'm hosting a fund-raising dinner Friday night, Hank," Wallace said as he walked with him to the door. "I'd like for you to attend and meet some people. It should help you with learning the business."

The idea of a fancy dinner didn't strike Hank as something he would enjoy, but he wasn't in the position to turn the man down. "Can I bring a friend?"

Wallace's white eyebrows raised. "Anyone in particular?"

"Elizabeth Edwards," Hank answered without hesitation.

"By all means, bring her along. I've met her a few times and found her to be a charming woman. Where did you meet her?"

Hank wasn't sure if he should be honest. What would his new boss think if he found out Hank had gone to an image consultant? "She's been advising me on how to get around in Kansas City," he hedged.

The knowing look he received assured him that Wallace knew the truth, but didn't care. Maybe she had had other clients who were employees. Not that Hank cared. But he did wonder how many had been as attracted to her as he was. And just how many had she been attracted to? Somehow, the thought made him uneasy.

"I'll stop by tonight, Mom." Lizzie propped the phone on her shoulder and shuffled through a list of prospective clients while she waited for her mother's reply.

"I'm sorry, Elizabeth. I just can't get around on my own yet."

Except for some slight lingering paralysis in her left side which would clear up in time, her mother was doing well. Still, she was weak from her time in the hospital and convalescent center. Lizzie felt the familiar guilt at not being there for her mother, but her business didn't always allow it. She wanted to help her mother, but she also wanted to prove to her family and her sister that she was now a responsible adult, not the wild teenager she had been.

Swallowing the familiar lump in her throat when she thought about the trouble she had caused her family, she answered with the only thing she could think of saying. "Maybe Vicky can help you until I can get there. I'm not able to leave right now, but I will be later."

"I don't mean to take you away from your business."

Lizzie laid the papers aside and massaged her temples. Between two calls from her sister and this one from her mom, she wasn't sure if she was going to be able to handle this. Vicky had suggested hiring a nurse, but Lizzie didn't know how they would afford it. She had known it wasn't going to be easy. Nothing had been since her dad had died three years ago.

"Don't worry about it, Mom. Really."

"I know your business is important to you, Elizabeth. As important as Victoria's family is to her. I just wish you could find a nice young man like your sister did. Then you could stay home with a family, and you wouldn't have to work so hard."

Lizzie couldn't help but notice the slur in her mother's voice, caused by the stroke. But even though the stroke had slowed her down, her mother's hopes hadn't changed, no matter what Lizzie did to try to explain that a family like Vicky's wasn't what she wanted. Vicky had always been the perfect daughter. Lizzie had been the disappointment.

"Amanda and I are fine, Mom. We don't need—"

She was interrupted by the buzz of the intercom, and Lizzie was forced to interrupt her. "Hang on one minute, Mom." Switching to the intercom line, she sighed. "What is it, Janine?"

"Hank Davis is on line two."

Hank? Why was he calling? It had taken her most of the weekend to regain her equilibrium and convince herself she was happy and ready to move on to her next client.

"Thanks, Janine." She tried to ignore the slight trembling of her hand when she pushed the button on the phone to reconnect with her mother. "Sorry, Mom, but I have to go."

"That's all right, Elizabeth. I'll do my best until you get here."

"Just don't overdo it," she cautioned. "I promise to come directly to your house, as soon as I can get away this afternoon. And if you need someone sooner, call Vicky."

"It's all right."

Shoving aside the guilt that always threatened to consume her when she spoke with her mother, she said goodbye and hung up. The big question now was why would Hank be calling her. She knew he'd had his first day of work and meeting with Daniel Wallace and suddenly wondered if something had gone wrong. Of course, she wasn't responsible for that, unless Hank didn't live up to Crown's expectations, and she doubted that. Even more, was she up to dealing with Hank, even over the phone? She knew the answer to that one. It was a simple *no,* but she didn't have a choice.

"Hank, this is Lizzie. Is something wrong?"

"There's been a major change in things."

She was shocked at the way her heart beat faster at the sound of his voice, but she tried to ignore it. "You still have the job, don't you?" She couldn't believe Daniel Wallace wasn't impressed with Hank. Then a thought struck her. "You didn't quit, did you?"

His soft chuckle sent electric currents through her. "Quit? No, nothing like that. Fact is, I've been offered a management position with Crown Construction. I don't know what got into the old man, but he seems to think my associate degree makes me the man for the job. Frankly I think he's lost his mind, but I figured I'd humor him. He's a nice old guy."

"That's wonderful, Hank!" She meant it. "But what does that have to do with me?"

She heard a slight hesitation before he spoke again. "There's this fund-raiser—a dinner—Friday night. I'd like it if you would go with me."

Dread mixed with eagerness snaked up her spine. An evening with Hank? Was he crazy? She had barely been able to get him out of her mind over the weekend. Seeing him again wasn't a good idea. "I don't know…"

"I'll even pay for your time."

Darn. The magic words. She only had one other client who wouldn't be able to start for another week, so it wasn't as if her time was taken up. Or that she had clients pounding her door for her services. But she couldn't take Hank's money. That would be wrong. Even so, she would be a fool to turn him down. The exposure would be good. Then again, she would be a fool if she agreed to go with him when she wasn't able to keep herself under control.

Hank's voice brought her back to the present. "I need some advice about clothes for this, Lizzie."

"A tuxedo," she answered automatically. "Fundraisers like this are always black tie." And she could just imagine Hank Davis in a tux. Who would help her keep her sanity?

"Lizzie, you still there?"

"All right," she said, wondering if she would live to regret agreeing to his invitation. "I have to work late, but I'll be happy to go to the dinner with you. Would you like for me to see if Bailey is available?"

"I'll call him. We'll pick you up at your office at seven on Friday. And, Lizzie? I owe you."

That was exactly what Lizzie was afraid of.

Seated in the limo on the way to the hotel for the fund-raising dinner, Lizzie sat across from Hank and hoped he didn't notice that she was checking him out. She hadn't seen him for a week, but by all appearances, he was getting along fine. Way too fine. Hank was too tempting.

"Do I pass inspection, Miss Edwards?" he asked, flicking at a spot of nothing on his tux lapel.

"As a matter of fact, you do," she answered, giving him a smile. "You look perfect, Hank. Are you accustomed to that new haircut yet?"

He shrugged and shifted in the seat, his discomfort clearly visible. "I don't mind the haircut. Learning how to do it right wasn't easy, but it's okay. It's this da— uh, darned tuxedo. Monkey suits just aren't my style."

If only he knew, Lizzie thought. He looked like a dream. Janine was right. He would be the most sought-after man in Kansas City, especially when women glimpsed him in the tux. And Lizzie was one of the least immune. She had tried—really tried—to force thoughts of him from her mind. But each time she reminded herself that she wasn't in the market for a man, a vision of him at the fitness center popped immediately to mind. Her hormones were completely out of control where he was concerned.

With an obviously exaggerated sigh, Hank held up his hands and inspected them. "I hope the guys on my crew in New Mexico never find out I had a manicure. They'd never let me live it down."

Lizzie took both his hands in hers, ignoring the wave of warmth that swept through her, and examined them closely. "I'm glad you had them done, but I had a feeling you might have gone out and dug in the dirt, just to spite me." She added a smile to soften the statement, not wanting to start another battle. "They certainly do pass inspection, and so do you." Releasing his hands, she fought the urge to rub her palms on her thighs to stop the tingling sensation that lingered. His charm was enough to deal with. Unfortunately for her, Hank had it all going for him—except his strong stubborn streak and his penchant for never staying in one place. During the course of their two weeks together, she'd learned enough about him to know that his freedom was important to him. A part of her admired him, but another part chided her for doing so.

"Here we are," she announced when the car

slowed and pulled into the driveway in front of the hotel. "Ready?"

The grimace on his face nearly made her laugh out loud. Poor Hank was out of his element. She hated to admit that she had missed working with him, but she was also relieved that she hadn't had to deal with her colliding emotions.

The uniformed doorman approached the limousine and opened the door. Hank got out first, then offered his hand to assist Lizzie. She hesitated a moment. *After tonight, life will definitely return to normal.* Bolstered by the thought, she took his hand, feeling the familiar warmth. She withdrew it as soon as she was on her feet outside the car.

In true gentlemanly fashion, Hank offered his arm. Just what she didn't need. She bit the inside of her cheek and offered a smile as she slipped her arm through his. It's nerves, she assured herself. Nothing more.

Once inside the building, they proceeded down the wide, marble-floored hallway, where she disengaged to remove her wrap. Staying true to form, Hank helped. As she turned to give him a grateful smile, they were hailed by their host from the doorway of the ballroom.

"Miss Edwards, you're looking lovely, as always."

She turned to the white-haired gentleman approaching them. "Thank you, Mr. Wallace. And thank you for the opportunity to join you tonight."

His long strides brought him to stand in front of them. "It's nice to see you. The dinner is for a good cause, but you'll hear more about that later." He reached out to grasp Hank's hand. "Glad you could join us tonight, Hank."

"Nice of you to have us both, sir," Hank replied as he shook Wallace's hand.

"I'll introduce you to some of the people you haven't met yet. Not only some of the best of Crown Construction, but from Wallace International and others, too." He turned to Lizzie. "You don't mind if I steal this young man from you for a bit and introduce him to a few friends, do you, Miss Edwards?"

For a brief moment, she saw a flash of panic in Hank's eyes, but it was gone as soon as she recognized it. "I'll meet you at our table, Hank," she told him, then turned to walk away. Behind her, she heard Daniel Wallace talking to him.

"We won't talk shop tonight, Hank. I like to enjoy these things. As much as possible, anyway."

She didn't catch Hank's reply, but she did hear his laughter before she moved out of earshot. Another small wave of relief. She was on her own, with the chance to mingle with people she didn't often get the chance to meet. It was a boost for her business, and since Amanda was spending the night with Vicky, she intended to take advantage of it.

Nearly thirty minutes later, she found her seat at the table and was joined by Hank, who wore his dimpled smile to perfection.

"You know, they're a nice bunch of people," he said, easing into the chair beside her. "More down-to-earth than I would've thought, what with all the money and power they wield."

"I'm glad you enjoyed yourself," she said, dropping her voice to a whisper as their host was introduced at the podium.

The man at the front of the room smiled benevolently on the room full of people to begin the evening.

"We've raised two hundred thousand dollars tonight, thanks to all of you, and special thanks to our friend and colleague, Daniel Wallace, for inviting us all."

Lizzie did her best to ignore the fact that Hank was sitting next to her. Each time he moved, their arms, legs or shoulders touched, and she had to fight off electric currents sparking through her veins. The speakers were entertaining, and the food was delicious, but thankfully the evening passed quickly. Lizzie found that, once again, she enjoyed Hank's company. And he seemed to have made an impression on everyone, especially Daniel Wallace, who appeared to have taken him under his wing.

She knew she shouldn't have enjoyed herself so much. The last man she had enjoyed spending time with had brought her heartache, causing her to swear off any kind of involvement. And here she was attracted to another unreliable man.

They had said their goodbyes to their dinner companions some minutes before and were nearing her office, where she had left her car. Hank had said very little since getting into the limo.

"Is something bothering you, Hank?"

"I guess the week has caught up with me," he answered with a shrug. He'd loosened his tie and the top studs of his tuxedo shirt, giving him an even more devil-may-care look than usual.

"That's not surprising. I think we did a great job, though."

"We?" His gaze met hers and held it.

Lizzie wanted badly to look away, but she couldn't. There was something in his eyes. Something she hadn't seen before. Something she wanted to know about, but knew she shouldn't. "I—I had an enjoyable time tonight."

His dimples were revealed with his smile. "Enjoyable? Why, Lizzie, does that mean you had fun?"

"Fun?"

"Like our pizza party. Can we do that again sometime?"

Lizzie couldn't deny that she had enjoyed the night they'd had pizza, but she couldn't let it become a habit. Amanda had talked of little else since then. Even Lizzie's mother had heard about Hank. It hadn't been an easy job convincing her mother that he was merely a client and not a prospective father for Amanda. How could Lizzie explain that Hank wasn't the type to stay around for long? And even if he had been, she wasn't interested. Couldn't be. Thank goodness her mother hadn't met him. And Amanda was doing fine, in spite of her new friendship with Hank. She was a happy, well-adjusted little girl again, and Lizzie didn't want anything to change that. She hadn't forgotten how hard it had been the last time, and she needed to nip this in the bud, for Amanda's sake.

"I can't imagine what's fun about eating pizza with a four-year-old," she said, hoping he caught the humor she was trying to convey. "Truthfully, Amanda had a good time, too. We both did," she added, softening the edge of what she needed to say next. "But I'd rather not make a habit of it. I don't want her to count on it being a regular activity."

His shrug was easy, but his frown deepened. "I guess you know what's right."

She hated being so callous, but her daughter's heart was at stake. Hers, too, if she wanted to be honest. But she didn't.

She was saved from having to think more about it when the car stopped. "Here we are," she said, relieved the night was nearly over.

"I'll walk you inside."

She couldn't think of a way to avoid him without appearing rude, so she simply nodded.

He got out and held the door for her, once again taking her hand to help her out of the car. "I'll just be a minute, Bailey."

"I'll be fine, Hank," she told him, wanting to escape even a short time alone with him. Once he was gone, she could work on phasing him out of her mind.

"Just using the things you taught me, Miss Edwards."

She heard the teasing in his voice, and felt the deep timbre there, too. Okay, she would get through this.

Her hand shook slightly as she fitted the key into the lock of the heavy, rough-hewn wooden door of Images, Inc. Inside, the office was dark and quiet. All she had to do was grab a couple of files she intended to take with her to her mother's house for the weekend.

Lost in her own thoughts, she didn't notice him moving to stand near her, until she nearly ran into him. Darn it! Even in the dark, when she couldn't see him, she could sense him. It unnerved her, and she hated that. Her battle to prove she wasn't the wild girl she'd once been wouldn't be won if he stayed around much longer.

"I'll get the light," she said, moving to switch it on. Instead of connecting with the lamp on Janine's desk, she connected with Hank, full force, her face hitting his chest.

The man was as solid as a brick wall. She couldn't

help but sway a little, and he put his hands on her arms to steady her. But just his touch unsteadied her.

"Lizzie..."

"Um, Hank, let me get the light."

She started to move away, but he held her. "No."

Instead of insisting, she held perfectly still. Waiting. She held her breath while fighting the wild child she realized still lived buried deep inside her. Her eyes had become accustomed to the dark, and she could see the white of his shirt, outlined by his jacket. But more than that, she heard his soft breathing, smelled the clean, musky scent of him, felt the warmth of his body. Her heart pounded. Not with fear, but with anticipation. She knew better than to let it go any further, but she couldn't stop herself. She couldn't stop anything.

"I'll go in a minute," he said, breaking the silence. "I only want to ask if you'd like to go to a movie or dinner or something tomorrow night. We can celebrate my new job. Or whatever."

"I—I can't."

"Amanda?"

She shook her head. "No. I have work to do this weekend." There. She'd said what she needed to say. No need to worry that she couldn't stay in control of herself and the situation. But much to her dismay, he still didn't release her.

She drew on every ounce of professionalism she had. "It's been a pleasure working with you, Hank. And I hope I helped you."

"Oh, you did."

For one moment, when he didn't say more, she thought that was the end of it. He would let her go, say good-night and be on his way. Exactly the way he should. But he didn't.

"Then I guess it won't matter if I do this," he said, his voice deep and rough in the darkness.

Before she knew what was happening, he drew her closer and lowered his head to press his lips against hers. At first, she was too surprised to react, but when he began deepening the kiss, it didn't take long for her to realize she was enjoying every bit of it.

She gained control enough to gather her wits just as he slowly, gently, ended the kiss and moved back, leaving her speechless and wanting more. She stood still, listening to his footsteps as he crossed the room to the door. He opened it, his broad shoulders silhouetted by the streetlights.

"Have you ever considered going into the torture business?" he asked.

She opened her mouth to answer something—anything—but he was gone before she could form a single word in her mind.

Chapter Five

Hank rang the doorbell and looked around. It was a nice neighborhood. The house was small, but he realized that Lizzie and her daughter probably wouldn't need much. Besides, who was he to know anything about houses? He'd spent most of his life in a camper or a pull-behind trailer. Even the few houses where he and his parents had lived for short periods hadn't been much to brag about—whatever had been cheap and relatively clean, at least while his mother had been living.

The door swung open to reveal Amanda, her curly hair sticking up in all directions and her mouth rimmed in purple. Grape jelly, of course.

"Hi, Hank! Want some bweakfast?"

"Thanks, Amanda, but I already—"

"Amanda, who's at the door?" Lizzie appeared behind her daughter, her mouth in a wide O when her gaze collided with his. "Hank. What are you doing here?"

He wasn't sure what had possessed him to hatch this plan. All he knew was that he wanted to surprise them. "It's such a beautiful day, I thought you ladies might want to share it with me."

"I do! I do!" Amanda piped up, bouncing up and down.

Lizzie's eyes narrowed and she hustled her daughter down the hallway, then returned to open the screen door and let him in. "I thought we discussed this last night," she said in an ominous whisper as he stepped inside.

There was no use pretending he didn't know what she was talking about. He had given it a lot of thought. He had it covered. "Did I mention pizza? Nope. I have something else in mind." He turned to look out the door he had just entered. "It's perfect."

"What's perfect?"

"The day."

"Hank, really—"

"Just a breeze in the air." Facing her again, he placed his hands on her shoulders and turned her around. "Better get Amanda dressed. I have a special surprise for her. For both of you."

"What do you think you're doing?"

Instead of answering, he followed her into the living room where they found Amanda sitting in front of the television. Cartoon characters danced across the screen. "Too much TV isn't good for kids," he said, picking up the little girl and tickling her. "She needs lots of fresh air."

"Hank—"

With a stroke of luck, the phone rang, forcing Lizzie to cross the room to answer it.

"Are you ready for an adventure, Amanda?" he asked as he set her on her feet.

She looked up at him, her eyes wide with wonder. "Like lion hunting in the jungle?"

"No, no lion hunting for us. Something much better."

Behind him, he could hear Lizzie's end of what sounded like a disagreement.

"But I told her I'd spend the day with her... No, Vicky, tell Dean that I have it covered. I'll be there in thirty minutes, as soon as I get the jelly off Amanda's face and tame her hair—" Her voice dropped. "Vicky, *pleeease*. Just let me do this today... I am not hiding anything. Why on earth would you think that?"

A furtive glance in Hank's direction was followed by the worst fake smile he had ever seen. She cupped her hand to the mouthpiece and quickly turned around, but he foiled her move by switching off the television.

"Take the boys to the movies or something," she continued. "Oh, all right. Have it your way. I'll be over later today... No, I do not owe you an explanation, and my behavior is not bizarre... Fine."

The sound of the receiver hitting the cradle echoed in the room. "So what is it that you have planned, Hank?" she asked when she turned around, her shoulders slumped in defeat.

"Fun," he answered, simply.

"Looky, Mommy, looky! It's touching the clouds!"

Hank took his attention off the kite long enough to turn around to see how Lizzie was taking all of this. The smile on her face filled him with more pleasure than he had ever known. Even the pleasure of surprising Amanda with the kite. He had never realized how a child's joy could spill over to affect others. He gazed down at the small creature with wonder. Whoever had fathered this child had his unending envy. Too bad he would never experience anything like it.

"Do you think you can hold on to the string by yourself?" he asked Amanda, leaning down to her level.

Her head bobbed up and down, but she never stopped watching the kite.

"Hold on real tight," he cautioned. "I'm going to go sit with your mom. If it starts to fall down, I'll be right back and we'll get it up and flying again."

"Okay."

Lizzie smiled at him when he took the spot beside her on the old army blanket he had won ten years before in a poker game. "Why do you know so much about having fun, Hank?"

He shrugged. "Guess I've had plenty of time to learn about it."

"Who taught you to fly a kite?"

A smile touched his lips as he remembered the day his dad had brought home the cheap plastic kite and ball of string. "My dad," he answered. "I couldn't have been much bigger than Amanda and didn't know what it was."

"You didn't know what a kite was? Oh, Hank."

When she reached over to touch his arm, he had to fight the urge to lay his hand on hers. He didn't want to scare her off. He had probably done enough of that already. "Hey, I could skip stones with the best of 'em."

"What kind of man was your father?"

"Hardworking." He turned to look at her. "Most people wouldn't believe that, if they knew the way we'd lived. I never had a permanent home. Not long enough to get attached to one, that is. Unless you want to call the pull-behind trailer we had for the last ten years a home. Most of the time it didn't bother me. Sometimes…"

"Sometimes what?" she asked, her voice gentle.

"That one kite was the only one I had that was store-bought. After that, he taught me how to make them out of newspapers and sticks. We tore up rags for the tail. And let me tell you, those homemade kites were better than that first one." He turned to watch Amanda tugging on the string as the kite dipped and bobbed in the sky. "I'll have to show Amanda how to make a newspaper kite."

"She'd like that."

Focusing on Lizzie, he couldn't miss the sparkle in her eyes or the roses in her cheeks. For the first time he could remember, she wasn't all bundled up in her usual suit or dressed to the nines. Instead she wore a pair of blue jeans, much like his, and a Kansas City Chiefs sweatshirt. Instead of tied up in a knot, her hair hung down her back in a single fiery braid. He wished she'd let it go, just once. But at least she was relaxed.

"And what would her mother like?" he couldn't help but ask.

The color in her cheeks deepened. "I don't know. To be able to have more time with Amanda, for one thing. She's growing up so fast."

"More time to have fun?"

Her gaze met his. "Yes, more time for fun. I—

well, ever since I opened Images, Inc., I've been so busy. Not that I mind," she hurried to assure him. "I want my business to be a success. But it has taken time away from Amanda." Her gaze moved to the small child holding the kite and she sighed softly. "But I guess that's something every single parent has to deal with. There's just never enough time for everything."

He wasn't sure if he should bring up the subject, but he knew she wouldn't answer if she didn't want to. Lizzie was a woman who didn't let anyone push her around. "What happened to her dad?"

She lowered her head and shook it. "He took off. I was just a kid. If it hadn't been for my family..." She shook her head again. "Sometimes I don't know how they put up with me."

Instead of continuing like he hoped she would, she jumped up. "Can I fly it, Amanda?" she shouted as she ran toward her daughter.

Hank didn't follow her. The scene before him was too beautiful to step into. He watched mother and daughter snuggling as they laughed at the kite dipping and diving in the breeze. Amanda would have wonderful memories of growing up. The thought made him glad he had his own few. And the memories of this day would last forever.

It was pretty clear that things hadn't always been easy for Lizzie. Whatever it was that had happened with Amanda's father had left scars. He knew everyone had scars, but he wondered if Lizzie's didn't go deeper than some. If he did nothing else during his stay in Kansas City, he would show Lizzie how to put the past behind her and enjoy life more.

* * *

Lizzie folded another towel and placed it on the pile. "If we could just make a schedule that would fit us both," she told her sister, picking up another towel.

Denny and Roger, her nephews, raced through her mother's kitchen with a screeching Amanda in their wake. Vicky lunged for the tower of towels to keep them from toppling. "Slow down, boys. Grandma is sleeping."

Lizzie grabbed the tail of Amanda's shirt and brought her to a halt. "Keep it down, sweetheart, or you three will have to take it outside."

"Can I show Denny and Woger my kite?" she asked, her blue eyes wide and innocent.

"You have a kite?" Vicky asked, as the two young boys let the outside door slam behind them. She shook her head. "I don't know what's gotten into them lately. It's like they don't hear a thing I say to them."

"They're just full of energy," Lizzie assured her, releasing Amanda and smoothing her hair. But even she had noticed how her nephews seemed to be testing her sister's limits. It wasn't at all like the boys. They were usually perfect gentlemen when they visited at their grandmother's house.

"Hank gave me a kite and teached me how to fly it," Amanda answered her aunt.

"Taught me," Lizzie corrected automatically and hoped it would interrupt her sister's train of thought. She cringed, knowing what was coming next if it didn't.

"Hank? Who's Hank?" Vicky asked.

"Hank is my new special fwiend."

"Someone at preschool, sweetie?"

"No. He's Mommy's special fwiend, too."

Vicky turned to give Lizzie a suspicious look. "You didn't tell me you were seeing someone."

"I'm not." Lizzie continued to fold the towel, hoping to hide how her hands had begun to tremble. Hank had shaken her up during their kite trip to the park the weekend before. When they'd reached her home, several hours later, she had once again reminded him that she didn't want Amanda counting on him too much. That had been four days earlier, and she hadn't heard from him since. She didn't expect to.

The back door flew open and Denny stuck his head inside. "Come on, Mandy Pandy! We found a bird's nest."

"Amanda," Lizzie called, as her daughter raced for the promise of a new adventure, "don't mess with the nest. The mommy birdie won't have anything to do with the babies if you bother their home."

"Okay," the little girl called over her shoulder, then followed her cousin outside.

Vicky started to follow her. "I swear, if those boys—"

"Leave them alone," Lizzie said. "We both know they'll all poke it with sticks and peer inside. They're just inquisitive."

"Yes, but—" She stopped, sighed and returned to the clothes. "With Dean working these long hours, the boys are getting more and more rambunctious."

"There's nothing wrong, is there?" Lizzie asked, sensing trouble. She loved her sister, in spite of her old feeling of inferiority and jealousy. It hadn't been easy growing up in Vicky's shadow. Having a sister who made straight A's and was one of the most popular girls in school had been more than Lizzie could deal with. Instead of simply forgetting about it and being herself, she had fought it and tried to gain attention in other ways. The wrong ways. Now that she was older, she understood some of what had caused her to choose the path she had when she was younger, and the two sisters had become close friends. Still, Lizzie couldn't forget the jealousy she had let turn her life in the wrong direction.

"Vicky?" she prodded.

"So who's this Hank?" Vicky asked, instead of answering the question.

"My latest client," Lizzie said, hoping this wouldn't turn into an interrogation. Since Amanda's birth, Vicky had been protective of both of them, especially when it came to men. Lizzie suspected it was because Vicky didn't want her to make another dreadful mistake. Lizzie assured her often that the sins of the past wouldn't be repeated, and she had learned a valued lesson. Still, Vicky watched after her.

"And he's a 'special fwiend'?" Vicky's grin reached from ear to ear. "Honestly, Lizzie, Amanda is so cute. I don't ever remember the boys being that cute. I've always been so envious of you."

Vicky envious? Lizzie stared at her sister.

But Vicky didn't notice and kept on talking. "What makes him so special?"

Shrugging, Lizzie grabbed the pile of clean towels, intending to escape by taking them to the bathroom. "I don't have the slightest idea."

Vicky laid a hand on her arm as she passed. "Amanda said he was your friend, too. Does this have anything to do with that bizarre conversation we had on the phone Saturday morning?"

Lizzie opened her mouth to deny it, but decided

that some kind of explanation was called for. If she denied it too strongly, Vicky's suspicions would be aroused, and Lizzie would never hear the end of it. "Hank is new in town and ended up sharing pizza with us the week before. Amanda took an instant liking to him."

"What's he like?"

Lizzie's face burned, and she hoped her sister didn't notice the blush she knew was there. She wasn't up to answering questions. Best to nip this in the bud before it went any further. "He's very nice, but from what I know of him, he isn't the type to stay around."

"Oh."

Lizzie heard the disappointment in her sister's voice. It was nothing compared to her own disappointment. Being attracted to Hank—and liking him as much as she did—was a battle she had to fight constantly. He had never once given her any indication that he was the type to settle down. Even with his adoration of Amanda and Lizzie's caution about breaking the little girl's heart, he had never mentioned anything about plans to stay in Kansas City. Changing a person's image was one thing. Changing a person was impossible. Lizzie knew that better than anyone.

She gave her sister a smile, then walked out of the room and down the hall to the bathroom. As she put the stack of fluffy clean towels in the cupboard, she heard the phone ring twice.

"Lizzie, the phone's for you," Vicky called from the hallway.

Lizzie closed the cupboard door and stepped into the hallway. "Who is it?"

"It's a man," Vicky whispered ominously and handed the phone to her.

"Probably Bailey wondering if I've found a new client." She put the phone to her ear. "Hello?"

"You're not an easy woman to track down," Hank said on the other end of the line.

Lizzie's heart skipped more than one beat, and she glanced at Vicky, who stood watching her with what was obviously clear expectation that something was up. "How did you know where to find me?"

"I couldn't reach you at the office or at home, so I called Bailey."

The traitor. She'd never thought to tell Bailey or Janine not to give Hank her mother's number. Feeling her sister watching and listening, she grabbed a tight hold on her professionalism. "Is there a problem?"

"Only if you don't say yes."

Heavens, what did the man have planned now? "No more pizza and kite flying," she warned.

Hank's laughter caused the threatening heat to climb a few degrees higher. "No, this has nothing to do with Amanda. I promised I would check with you first before planning anything."

"Thank you. That means a lot. So what is it?"

"Daniel has invited us both for dinner on Friday night."

The familiarity in his voice surprised her. "Daniel? You're on a first-name basis with your boss?"

"Well, we seem to be getting along well. He's a nice old guy, Lizzie. Kind of lonely. And he's been real generous with his time and all the help he's given me on the job. Like it's important to him that I do okay."

Lizzie had suspected that Daniel Wallace had taken

to Hank. With the few things Hank had casually said at the park and on the way home, it had seemed that Daniel was keeping an eye on him. It certainly wouldn't hurt Hank. Having someone with as much power as Daniel Wallace in his corner could mean big things down the road. *If* Hank stuck around. And whether Lizzie wanted to admit it or not, she hoped he would. If going to dinner with him meant that was a possibility, she wouldn't refuse.

"What time on Friday?"

He gave her the details, while Lizzie wondered what she was getting herself into. She didn't want to get her hopes up, any more than she wanted Amanda thinking that Hank might become a more permanent fixture in their lives. She knew better than to count on anyone. Besides, she knew what she wanted in life, and it didn't include Hank or any other man.

When she had said goodbye and hung up the phone, she turned to see her sister's smile. "Don't get any ideas," she warned Vicky, "but I've been invited to have dinner at Daniel Wallace's home."

"I think I need to meet this Hank," Vicky said with a grin.

The idea terrified Lizzie. She had never made a habit of bringing men home to meet her family. "We'll see."

Vicky snapped her fingers. "Darn. I forgot to tell you."

"What?"

Pulling out a chair, Vicky pointed to it. "You'd better sit down."

Concerned by the look on her sister's face, Lizzie did as she was told. "What is it? You look... Well, whatever it is, I'm not sure I want to know."

"And I hate to tell you, but forewarned is forearmed," she said, pulling out another chair for herself.

Vicky's lips were set in a grim line, and Lizzie's heart thudded with fear. "Is it Mom?"

Shaking her head, Vicky took a deep breath. "When was the last time you heard from Jeffrey?"

"Jeffrey?" Lizzie's heart stopped. "The day I told him I was pregnant. Why?" Panic threatened to overwhelm her. No one had spoken of Jeffrey since Amanda's birth.

Vicky lowered her head, licked her lips, then looked up. "I saw him yesterday. At least I think it was him. He hasn't contacted you?"

Unable to speak, Lizzie shook her head. Jeffrey was the last person she expected to hear from. The last person she wanted to hear from. Maybe Vicky was wrong. Maybe it had only been someone who looked like Jeffrey. Still, she would have to be on guard.

"This is wonderful brisket, Mr. Wallace," Lizzie told their host. "I'd love to have the recipe."

"Martha is a wonderful cook," he replied. "Worth her weight in gold as a friend, too. She's been with the family for years and stayed when my wife died. I don't think I could've managed without her. I'll introduce you both to her before she leaves for the night. She's taking some time off to visit her sister in St. Louis."

Hank sat across the table from Lizzie and listened to the exchange as the two discussed culinary favorites. As far as he was concerned, a thick, juicy steak, cooked to perfection, and a baked potato heaped with sweet butter and sour cream were his idea of the best meal. Half the things they mentioned were completely foreign to him, and there was no sense showing his ignorance. If he decided to stay in Kansas City for any length of time, it might be best if he sampled some of the fancy meals they talked about.

He was beginning to lean toward giving the city and his job a try. Six months seemed fair, if that's what he decided to do. But he hadn't told anyone yet, not even Lizzie. As difficult as it was for him to admit, she was a big part of the reason he was considering it.

"Ah, here's Martha now," Daniel said and rose to his feet, when a gray-haired woman stepped into the room.

Remembering his manners and following his host's lead, Hank stood and waited for introductions.

"Martha, I'd like for you to meet Elizabeth Edwards," Daniel said, bestowing a smile upon Lizzie. "She owns an image consulting business here in Kansas City and is quite a bright young lady, from what I've heard."

"So nice to meet you, Miss Edwards," Martha replied. "And what a lovely sweater you're wearing."

Color rushed into Lizzie's cheeks. "Why thank you. I told Daniel that I don't think I've ever had brisket prepared so well. Will you share your secret with me?"

It was Martha's turn to blush. "Oh, it's nothing much," she said with a dismissive wave of her hand. "I enjoy cooking so much because it gives me the chance to try something a little new now and then. Daniel can tell you that it doesn't always turn out for the best, but I haven't poisoned him yet."

Hank joined in the laughter, then Daniel turned in his direction. "And this is Hank Davis, Martha."

Something in her eyes caught Hank's attention. The emotion in them was impossible to read, but it was almost as if—

"So this is Hank," she said, her smile widening with pleasure. "Daniel has told me so much about you, I almost feel as if we've met. It's wonderful to have you here. I hope you enjoyed your dinner?"

"Very much," he said, honestly. "And it's a pleasure to meet you, too." As she stood looking at him, her face beaming, his collar seemed to tighten around his neck. Introductions. He hated introductions and never knew what to say. Lizzie had tried to help and, according to her, he'd done very well, but when it came right down to it, the right words never came to mind.

Daniel touched her arm. "Maybe we'll have dessert now, before you leave."

"Let me help," Lizzie said, placing her napkin on the table and scooting her chair back to stand. "Maybe a little of your culinary skills will wear off on me."

Martha laughed. "There's really nothing to it, and I'll be happy to share. And I certainly welcome your company in the kitchen." She turned to Hank. "It was so nice to meet you, Hank. I do hope we see more of you here."

Hank mumbled what he hoped was an appropriate reply. When the women had gone, he took a drink of water from the crystal glass at his plate, then cleared his throat. "She must be like a part of your family."

"She is. She was married when she first came to work for us. She and Ida became good friends in a short time. Then Martha's husband died suddenly, so she stayed. She's lived here in her own apartments since. She—well, I'll tell you more later," he finished, as the women returned with plates of some sort of chocolate and cherry concoction.

When Lizzie had settled back at the table, Martha bid them goodbye. "I'll be back on Wednesday, Daniel. You have my sister's number, if you need me."

After Martha left the room, Hank enjoyed the dessert and the conversation as he and Daniel compared notes on various areas of the country.

"Tell me about your family, Miss Edwards," Daniel said as they finished.

For a brief second, Lizzie's eyes clouded, then she smiled. "I'm the middle of three children. An older sister, Victoria, who's happily married and has two delightful boys. My brother, Richard, is younger and attends college in Chicago. I lost my father to heart failure three years ago, but he was a well-respected teacher in the English department at Pem Hill." She turned to Hank. "That's Pembroke Hill, a private school here in Kansas City."

"Pem Hill?" Daniel asked. "Ida attended Sunset Hill before the schools merged, and my daughter was a student at Pem. Where did you go to school?"

"Pem," Lizzie answered, her voice strangely quiet. "We were allowed admission since my father taught there."

Daniel seemed to catch on that this was a topic Lizzie wasn't eager to discuss, because he quickly changed the subject. "Is your mother still living?"

Lizzie nodded and seemed to relax. "She suffered a stroke four months ago, but she's doing much better now."

"Nasty things, strokes," Daniel said. "But Hank tells me you have a daughter. How old is she?"

"She's four."

"Hank says she's a delight."

The smile she gave Hank touched his heart. Amanda was one bundle of joy, but her mother had come to mean even more to him. A dangerous situation, he knew, and he had to constantly remind himself that he wasn't husband material for her or any other woman. Staying put was not one of his strong points. Even if it had been, he didn't know the first thing about being a family man. And as far as he was concerned, it was too late to learn.

"She's a wonder," Lizzie answered, her voice full of motherly pride. "But I wasn't aware that you had a daughter."

Daniel was silent, then stood and moved away from the table. "Let's go into my study for drinks and coffee. I'd like to show you both something."

"Maybe I should get the dishes," Lizzie offered, "since Martha will be gone."

"No, no need for that," Daniel told her, motioning for them to follow. "Getting them to the kitchen later will give me something to do. I have someone coming in tomorrow to help while she's gone."

As Daniel led them from the dining room, Hank followed behind the two and didn't fail to notice the inviting sway of Elizabeth's hips. With each step she took, his urge to plant his hands on either side and pull her close grew. When it got to be more than he could handle, he took a deep breath, let it out slowly, and turned his attention to his surroundings.

Daniel Wallace lived in the lap of luxury. Hank couldn't imagine living in something he could only think of as a mansion. The estate seemed to run on and on for miles, and the house was huge and silent. Their footsteps didn't make a sound on the plush carpeting, and he wondered if laughter had ever filled the house that now felt like a tomb. How long had it been this way? In that instant, he was glad for the life he had led, in spite of having to do without for most of his life.

Opening a door, Daniel ushered them into a paneled room. "That's my Ida," he said, indicating an almost life-size portrait of a woman hanging on the wall behind a massive desk.

Hank stared at the portrait. Her deep brown eyes were kind in a beautiful face, but something about the woman bothered him. Something was vaguely familiar.

"And over here," Daniel said, crossing the room to a lighted niche in the wall, "is my daughter."

Hank stopped breathing, but managed one word. "No."

Chapter Six

Elizabeth heard pain and denial in Hank's voice and turned to look at him. "Hank? Is something wrong?" Her answer was clear when she saw the look on his face. Something was very wrong. Crossing the room, she placed her hand on his arm. "What is it?"

Instead of answering her, he jerked away and strode toward Daniel. "Is this some kind of sick joke?"

"Hank—" she began.

"Stay out of this, Lizzie," he said, without looking at her. He continued to stare at Daniel, who had paled. "Where did you get that picture?"

Daniel's face was unreadable in the dim light of the study. "That's a picture of my daughter."

A muscle in Hank's jaw worked. "No, that's a picture of my mother. How did you get it?"

Lizzie bit her lower lip to keep from gasping aloud. She saw the tension mounting in his rigid body. The atmosphere in the room was quickly becoming volatile. "Why don't we all sit down and talk about this? I'm sure there's a reasonable explanation."

He turned on her. "Reasonable explanation? I'd like to hear any explanation he has for this." Darting a menacing glance at Daniel, he allowed Lizzie to lead him to a leather sofa against one wall. He waited until Daniel settled in a matching leather wing chair. "Okay, let's hear it."

Daniel sat silent for a moment, studying Hank. "You look like her, you know."

Angrily waving a dismissive hand, Hank shook his head. "That's not the point. I want to know how you got your hands on a picture of my mother. Or of someone who *looks* like my mother."

Lizzie placed her hand on his, hoping it would in some way calm him. "Give him time," she whispered. "I know this is hard for you, but it must be hard for him, too."

Hank stared at her as if in complete disbelief that she could think of how Daniel might be feeling at the moment. The hard look in his eyes softened. He turned his hand over and wrapped his fingers around hers, giving it a squeeze. "I just feel like I've been hit with a ton of bricks," he told her in a low voice.

"I know," she replied, answering his squeeze with one of her own. "But give him a chance. Hear him out."

After a slight hesitation, he nodded and turned his attention to Daniel. "My mother always told me she didn't have any family."

"That doesn't surprise me," Daniel said with a sad smile. "Your mother was always very headstrong. It's a good quality—"

"What makes you so certain that your daughter was my mother?"

"What's your middle name?"

Hank pressed his lips together as he lowered his head. "Wallace."

"You never knew it was her maiden name?"

Shaking his head, Hank looked at him. "No, never."

Daniel shifted in his chair.

Lizzie found a flaw in this. "Hank, didn't you wonder when you met Daniel?"

"Wallace is a fairly common name."

"But you knew your mother was from Kansas City," she pointed out. "Didn't that make you curious, at least?"

"If you'd known my mother, known how we lived—" He shook his head. "It didn't add up. It doesn't add up now. Why would she tell me she didn't have any family when she did?"

Daniel cleared his throat. "When your mother left here, it was under strained circumstances. We'd had an argument. I'd said things I shouldn't have, and she took them to heart. Obviously more to heart than I would ever have imagined."

Hank asked the question Lizzie wanted to ask. "What did you argue about?"

The shadow that fell over Daniel's face and his hesitation made it clear the question wasn't one he wanted to answer. "I wasn't in favor of the young man she was seeing."

Hank sat up straighter. "Who was that?"

Daniel seemed to be battling with himself. "There are a few things you need to understand, Hank."

"Who was he?" Hank repeated.

Lowering his head, Daniel took a deep breath, then raised his head to look directly at Hank. "Your father."

Hank jumped to his feet. "My *father?*"

Lizzie could only imagine how Hank felt. She had learned how much he thought of the man who had raised him after his mother had died. This was a direct hit to his heart. Still, she knew she must calm him down so Daniel could explain. Surely there was an explanation.

"Sit down, Hank," she said, tugging at his hand. "Let Daniel finish. Please."

"As far as I'm concerned—" He looked down at her and the fight seemed to go out of him. "Okay."

When he had settled once again on the sofa next to her, Daniel continued. "I've learned a lot in the past thirty-two years, son."

Beside her, Hank tensed. She squeezed the hand that was wrapped tightly around hers and prayed this would end well, for both Hank and Daniel.

"What's that?" Hank asked.

"I've learned that a person's background has little to do with whether he's a good man or not. I should have known that, having come from a lower middle-class family myself."

"You?" Hank asked. "I don't believe it."

"I left home as a young man, out to make a million dollars."

"And you made twenty times over that," Lizzie said in awe.

Daniel shook his head. "It made a difference in how I looked at things. But I lost the things that meant the most to me. First Ida shortly after Marjorie's birth, then Marjorie."

The Silhouette Reader Service™ — Here's how it works:

Accepting your 2 free books and mystery gift places you under no obligation to buy anything. You may keep the books and gift and return the shipping statement marked "cancel." If you do not cancel, about a month later we'll send you 6 additional books and bill you just $3.34 each in the U.S., or $3.80 each in Canada, plus 25¢ shipping & handling per book and applicable taxes if any.* That's the complete price and — compared to cover prices of $3.99 each in the U.S. and $4.50 each in Canada — it's quite a bargain! You may cancel at any time, but if you choose to continue, every month we'll send you 6 more books, which you may either purchase at the discount price or return to us and cancel your subscription.

*Terms and prices subject to change without notice. Sales tax applicable in N.Y. Canadian residents will be charged applicable provincial taxes and GST. Credit or Debit balances in a customer's account(s) may be offset by any other outstanding balance owed by or to the customer.

NO POSTAGE
NECESSARY
IF MAILED
IN THE
UNITED STATES

BUSINESS REPLY MAIL
FIRST-CLASS MAIL   PERMIT NO. 717-003   BUFFALO, NY

POSTAGE WILL BE PAID BY ADDRESSEE

SILHOUETTE READER SERVICE
3010 WALDEN AVE
PO BOX 1867
BUFFALO NY 14240-9952

If offer card is missing write to: Silhouette Reader Service, 3010 Walden Ave., P.O. Box 1867, Buffalo NY 14240-1867

Get FREE BOOKS and a FREE GIFT when you play the...

LAS VEGAS GAME

Just scratch off the gold box with a coin. Then check below to see the gifts you get!

YES! I have scratched off the gold Box. Please send me my **2 FREE BOOKS** and **gift for which I qualify.** I understand that I am under no obligation to purchase any books as explained on the back of this card.

▼ DETACH AND MAIL CARD TODAY! ▼

© 2001 HARLEQUIN ENTERPRISES LTD.
® and TM are trademarks owned by Harlequin Enterprises Ltd.

315 SDL DUYE   **215 SDL DUYU**

FIRST NAME

LAST NAME

ADDRESS

APT.#

CITY

STATE/PROV.

ZIP/POSTAL CODE

(S-R-04/03)

7	7	7	Worth TWO FREE BOOKS plus a BONUS Mystery Gift!
🍒	🍒	🍒	Worth TWO FREE BOOKS!
🔔	🔔	♣	TRY AGAIN!

Visit us online at **www.eHarlequin.com**

Offer limited to one per household and not valid to current Silhouette Romance® subscribers. All orders subject to approval.

Because Hank was silent and apparently considering Daniel's confession, Lizzie asked the next question. "What happened after your argument with your daughter?"

"By the next morning, I had calmed down enough to be rational. But I still believed her love for James Davis was nothing more than an adolescent crush. Because she had always been so headstrong, I thought she had chosen him to irritate me."

Understanding, Lizzie nodded. "To push your buttons."

"Exactly."

"But you were wrong," Hank said. "Did you even know my father? Did you know what kind of man he was?"

"No, I never did," Daniel admitted. "At one point, I was able to locate them. I tried to contact her. I knew I had made a mistake and I wanted to apologize. I tried to do that. Several times, in several letters. Every one of them was returned, unopened. Then I lost track of them again."

"So you just gave up."

Daniel smiled wryly. "If you think Wallace is a common name, try finding someone named James Davis." Rubbing a hand across his eyes, he sighed. "But at the time, yes, I gave up. By the time I did locate some information a second time, Marjorie was gone and so was he. You were grown and had moved on."

Lizzie's heart was breaking for both men. Daniel had carried more than his share of guilt for too many years. Hank had the chance to make the situation easier, but his anger and resentment were keeping him from seeing the truth. Daniel had made a mistake—a mistake that many parents had made and would continue to make in the future. She was thankful her parents had reacted differently to her situation. If only she knew what to say to make Hank understand. Before she could think of the right words, Hank pulled his hand from hers and moved away. She knew enough about body language to know that he was closing himself off by putting distance between himself and the person closest to him. He needed her help more than ever, but she didn't know how or what to offer.

"I have one more question," Hank said, getting to his feet. "Did I receive the letter offering me the foreman's job at Crown Construction because I was your..."

"Grandson?" Daniel finished. "That's a difficult question to answer. I wasn't certain you were Marjorie's son. There was a lapse of several years before I located you. I wasn't sure it was you, but I did hope you were my grandson. Everything I'd learned through a private investigator pointed to you."

"So the job offer—and the management job—are because of who I am, not because of my qualifications."

"No. Not completely. You've grown into a fine man," Daniel said in a strong voice. "It's obvious that Wallace blood runs through your veins."

"Davis blood, too," Hank said, a note of challenge in his voice.

Daniel shook his head, as if to dismiss the fact. "From what I know of you, I'd say it's the Wallace that's made you the man you are today."

"And just what do you know?" Hank asked.

"Everything."

"Then you know how hard life was for us."

"I didn't know at the time. I did what I could when I found her. She could have come home, she could have come to me and asked for help. But she was young and headstrong. She made the choice not to answer my letters. You have no idea how many times I wish I had done things differently."

Hank stood silently, unmoving.

"What's your choice?" Daniel asked. "Will you continue to work for Crown Construction? Or will you let your pride destroy you, as it has our family?"

Hank raised one shoulder and let it fall. "Depends."

"A smart man wouldn't throw away an opportunity like this. You're a smart man, Hank."

"Maybe even smarter than you think. I know one thing you don't. One thing you're wrong about. My parents weren't proud. My mother, least of all. We were happy, even though we didn't have anything like all of this." Hank waved his arm in a circle, and the gesture included more than the room. It encompassed a lifestyle that even Lizzie had never aspired to. "It's pretty obvious to me that things—wealth—didn't make her happy," he continued. "Still, if you had only accepted my father. If you had given him a chance. But you didn't, and maybe because of that, she died too young. She refused to go to the hospital with pneumonia because we didn't have insurance."

Watching Daniel's expression, Lizzie knew Hank had wounded the man. Her heart sank. Daniel had reached out to him, had admitted that he had been at fault, but Hank wanted to lay the blame for everything at Daniel's door. Lizzie couldn't agree with that.

She stood and reached out to place her hand on

Hank's arm. "Don't you see, Hank? We all make mistakes. Daniel is trying to make up for his."

"Maybe it's too late for that," he said, then turned back to Daniel. "I'll let you know if I plan to stay with the job. I need to think about all of this."

Daniel's answer was a nod.

"We'll find our way out." Hank held his hand out to Lizzie. "Come on. It's late, and Bailey will be waiting."

As they walked down the gravel path to the waiting limo, Lizzie turned to Hank. "He was only—"

"Not now," he cut her off, opening the car door before Bailey could do it. He waited until they were inside and had driven away from the estate. "You can't help me with this, Lizzie. There isn't anything you can teach me about how to deal with this."

Lizzie knew he was right, but she wondered if there wasn't something she could do. Somehow, she needed to show him that people made mistakes. If he couldn't accept that, how would he ever accept her?

Hank parked the rental car at the curb of the address Lizzie had given him. If he could have refused her invitation without hurting her feelings, he would have. But she had made it clear when she called him the day before that if he didn't come, she not only would be angry, she would be disappointed. He might not care if she was mad at him. He could deal with that and find a way to get back in her good graces again. But he couldn't disappoint her.

He sat staring at the empty street in front of him and drummed his fingers on the steering wheel. When had it become important that he not disappoint Lizzie? That sort of thing had never mattered before.

The only person, other than his parents, he had ever cared that he didn't disappoint was himself. Looking back, he had only done that a few times, and he had learned a lesson from each one. But now Lizzie had entered the equation. This wasn't how this was supposed to go.

Glancing at the two-story house where he knew she was waiting for him, he was tempted to start the car and drive away. Wasn't that what a man like him would do? No ties, he had always vowed. People left. People died. He had seen what losing someone had done to his dad. The depression. The drinking that had grown worse as each year went by, until James Davis had ceased to exist, even before his death. And all because of love.

And yet Hank couldn't disappoint Lizzie.

He still hadn't been able to come to terms with the fact that Daniel Wallace was his grandfather, although it had only been two days. Maybe in time he could, but would he ever think of his mother in the same way?

Opening the car door, he got out and slowly made his way to the house. He didn't love Lizzie. He couldn't. What could he give her? What could he do for her? He didn't have a clue how to relate to a woman. He'd spent most of his young life with his dad, and the rest on his own, surrounded by men. Women—how they acted, how they thought—were foreign to him. And he knew it was important to understand those things if he chose to have a relationship with someone. He had listened to enough talk among his fellow workers to know that. Instead of taking the opportunities that had come along throughout his life, he had chosen to go it alone.

Standing at the front door of Lizzie's mother's home, ready to push the doorbell, he realized he was thinking in circles. He hadn't made a decision about his job at Crown because he hadn't made a decision about Lizzie. He didn't understand why her opinion had become so important to him. He didn't understand why he couldn't disappoint her.

The idea that she would mean so much scared him. In that split second, he knew he couldn't face her. Not today. Maybe not ever again.

He turned and started down the wide porch steps, shoving his hands into his pockets. He was halfway to his car when he heard the door behind him open.

"Hank? Where are you going?"

The question was one his mother had asked a million times. As he had then, he stopped. Turning, he saw Lizzie standing in the doorway. A beam of sunlight had slipped through the shadows to set her hair afire.

"Forgot my keys," he answered, unsure of what to do.

"Oh, okay. I thought you were leaving."

Deciding he had to go through with his visit, he quickened his steps and hurried to his car, retrieved his keys, then returned to meet her on the porch. "Bad habit I need to break," he said as she ushered him inside.

"Everyone is out back. We're about ready to eat."

Her voice held a cheerful note, but he didn't miss the worry lines between her eyes. Had she been worried he wouldn't show up?

"Sorry I'm late," he mumbled.

She led him through the house where delicious aromas made his mouth water. "Don't worry about it.

We're always running late when it comes to dinnertime. I hope you brought your appetite. Mom and Vicky have made enough for an army, as usual.''

At the rear of the house, they stepped out onto a redwood deck. A few steps below them, Hank could see Lizzie's family gathering around a large wooden picnic table piled high with food.

"Denny, you and Roger get your hands washed," a young woman who resembled Lizzie called to two young boys. Hank guessed she was Lizzie's sister and the boys must be the infamous Denny and Roger.

The brothers raced up the steps and past Hank and Lizzie. Behind them, like a miniature tornado, Amanda followed, but came to a teetering halt when she saw Hank. Throwing her arms around his legs, she hugged him.

"Mommy thought you weren't coming," she told him. "But I knew you would be here."

"Got caught in road construction."

Looking up at him, Amanda's smile widened. Without another word, she scampered after her cousins. Watching her, he realized that Lizzie wouldn't have been the only one he would have disappointed if he had gotten in his car and driven away. Suddenly he was glad Lizzie had caught him.

"You must be Hank," a man in his mid-thirties said, coming up the steps to offer his hand. "I'm Dean Jacobs, Vicky's husband. Not a day goes by we don't have some kind of road construction slowing us down."

Hank took the offered hand and accepted the warm welcome. "So I'm learning."

Dean gave him a friendly slap to the back and turned to Lizzie. "I'll introduce Hank to everyone.

Your mom said to bring the chicken out, then we can eat."

Hank hated to see her disappear into the house, leaving him with a group of people who were complete strangers. But her brother-in-law quickly made him feel comfortable as they discussed Kansas City traffic and drivers.

"So you're the mysterious Hank," her sister said, approaching them with a warm smile. "It's so nice to meet you. I'd say Lizzie has told us all about you, but it would be a lie. In fact, when grilled, she's said very little. I'm glad my curiosity is finally being satisfied."

"I've heard enough about you to make me curious, too," Hank said.

"That doesn't surprise me," she said with a laugh. "Lizzie has been very mysterious lately. But enough about that. Come meet Mom." She looped her arm with his and led him to the table where an older woman fussed over the paper napkins that threatened to blow away in the breeze. "Mom, this is Lizzie's Hank."

When the woman looked up with a welcoming smile, he noticed the slight droop on one side of her mouth. Lizzie had mentioned that her mother had suffered a stroke and was slowly recovering from it. From what he could see, she was doing fine.

Her blue eyes twinkled as she reached out to take his hand and give it a pat with the other. "We're so glad you could make it, Hank. Elizabeth was ready to start eating, but I told her we'd wait a little longer. The beans weren't done anyway."

"Kansas City traffic," Dean said, coming up behind them to slip an arm around his wife's waist. "I wish she'd hurry with that chicken, or I'll have to send you in after her," he told his wife.

Mrs. Edwards gave Hank's hand a final pat before releasing him. "Here she comes now, Dean. Hank, why don't you sit over here?"

"I wanna sit next to Hank!" Amanda raced around her mother, who was balancing a huge platter piled high with golden chicken, to climb onto the bench next to him. "Mommy can sit on the other side. He's *our* fwiend." She gave her cousins, who were scrambling onto the bench across from them, a triumphant smile.

Hank immediately understood why Lizzie had said Amanda could take care of herself where her cousins were concerned. He chuckled to himself. Amanda was a lot like her mother.

The others took their places at the table, offered a blessing for their bounty and passed around plates and bowls laden with food. Conversations mingled and wove around to include everyone. Hank was questioned in a friendly way about his opinion of Kansas City, his travels and what he thought of Lizzie's business. He gave the latter high marks.

"She knows what she's doing," he told them all. "Look at what she's done for me. I came here with the prospect of a job as a foreman and no family, and in less than four weeks, I'm not only an office manager, I've gained a grandfather."

It was out of his mouth before he realized he had made a joke about his situation. It surprised him even more that he admitted to his relationship to Daniel Wallace. He knew why. Lizzie's family held no pretensions. They were good, down-to-earth people who had welcomed him as if he were one of them. By the time they finished the meal, he had made several friends. There was no way he could thank them for their friendship.

Everyone helped remove what little uneaten food was left and to clear the debris from the table. Even Dean and the boys did their share of work. Without wondering if he should or what needed to be done, Hank pitched in, too.

When they had finished, the women settled at the table, while the cousins took turns on the two swings. Hank leaned against a tree near the table and watched. Although he knew he shouldn't, he wished his life had included a family like the Edwards. He reminded himself that his childhood had been a happy one, even for a few years after his mother's death. Their lives had been different, but not bad.

"Join us for a walk around the block?" Dean asked him. Vicky let out a groan of protest as he tugged her to her feet.

Hank looked to Lizzie for an answer, but couldn't read her expression.

"We'll catch up with you in a few minutes," she said. As the couple walked away, she stood and turned to Hank. "It's a family tradition," she said with a shrug. "My mom and dad started it when they were courting. When we kids came along, we went along, too."

"Is your mom coming, too?" He had noticed that Mrs. Edwards was no longer in the yard with them.

"She's resting. This is the first family get-together since she had the stroke," she explained. "She's happy, but tired. And she really took a liking to you, Hank."

Before he could tell if Lizzie was pleased with that

or if it bothered her, she turned and moved away. It shouldn't matter to him, but it did.

Shoving away from the tree, he followed her. "Let's take that walk," he said, hoping he could discover what she was thinking.

She watched Amanda skip off after the Jacobs, who called to Lizzie and Hank, inviting them to follow. "You don't have to join us. I know we can be overwhelming."

"Are you trying to discourage me?" he asked, taking her hand. She shook her head and smiled, sending a not-so-welcome feeling of relief through him. He ignored it. "Good. There's one thing you need to know. I'm not one to spit in the face of tradition."

As they reached the corner of the house and headed for the sidewalk, Lizzie stayed beside him, but kept a good foot of space between them. "Does that mean you've decided to stay at Crown?"

"That's not the same thing." When she started to argue, he continued. "But that doesn't mean I've made a decision. I'm still considering it."

"I'm glad. I think."

Laughing, he reached for her hand. When she attempted to pull away, he held firm. "They're holding hands," he pointed out, nodding in the direction of Dean and Vicky.

"They're an old married couple," she answered. "They might get the wrong idea if they saw us doing the same."

"I think they've already gotten the wrong idea," he said, grinning.

"Only because they all think I should find a man and settle down."

"And what do you think?" He wasn't sure what

he wanted her to answer. He looked at the couple ahead of them and felt an unwelcome pang of envy. What the Jacobs and many others had, he never could. He was the son of a drifter who often changed jobs with the season and enjoyed life. He was a man who had never had roots. Putting them down now would be an effort in frustration. And probably failure. Still, it mattered to him what Lizzie hoped for in her future.

"I don't know," she said, after they had walked for some time. "People say children need a father. But Amanda is fine. She has a full, happy life. A family who loves her. Thanks to Dean, she hasn't missed having a dad. Maybe that's enough."

Hank came to a stop in the middle of the sidewalk and turned Lizzie to face him. "I didn't ask about Amanda."

Emotions crossed her face with lightning speed and finally settled on a smile. "I don't think much about myself, Hank. I worry about Amanda. That's my first job. If I really believed she needed a father, I would have gotten her one, long before now."

"You need to think of yourself first, Lizzie."

She shook her head. "No, I'm doing fine. But maybe now you can understand why I don't want her getting too attached to you. Two years ago she formed an attachment to someone else—a man who didn't want a ready-made family. Now she's at the age when little girls bond with their daddies. I don't want her bonding with a man who won't be here for the long run. I have to protect her from that."

Hank understood more than she knew. "And you want to protect yourself, too, don't you? Why?"

She took a step away from him. "There's a lot you don't know."

"So tell me," he called to her when she turned to continue the walk.

"There's no reason to do that."

Hank knew better than to push her. If Lizzie wasn't willing to share with him, there wasn't anything he could do. He understood that she needed stability and a normal home. It wasn't something familiar to him. Or natural. He couldn't make a commitment, but he couldn't walk away from her, either.

"Can I still spend time with both of you?" he asked.

"Oh, Hank..."

"No, hear me out. I'll take full responsibility for Amanda," he said, hoping he could do it. "I'll talk to her, explain the situation, let her know that she and I are 'fwiends' and nothing more. Would she understand?"

"I'm not sure, but I don't see that I have an option," she answered as Amanda came running to join them.

"Denny and Woger and Aunt Vicky and Uncle Dean are going to the zoo next weekend. Can I go wif them?"

"Why don't we all go?" Hank suggested. "You and your mommy and me." This would be the perfect opportunity for him to have a little talk with Amanda and explain things to her. He didn't want to leave her high and dry any more than her mother wanted it to happen.

Amanda's eyes grew round, then she jumped up and down. "Yes! Yes! That would be even more fun!"

Before either Hank or Lizzie had a chance to say

anything, she ran to tell her cousins the news. Lizzie turned to Hank. "I hope you know what you're doing."

Hank hoped he did, too.

Chapter Seven

Pleading a headache and cranky boys, Vicky and her family begged off on the trip to the zoo, leaving Lizzie and Amanda with Hank. Amanda was in her element. Perched atop Hank's shoulders so she had a perfect view of the animals, her face glowed with happiness. From a distance, Lizzie watched as her daughter mimicked the chimpanzees and giggled with joy, until she noticed the mustard trailing down Amanda's arm from the hot dog she held and threatening to drip on Hank's shirt.

Hurrying over with a napkin to dab at the yellow streak, Lizzie hated to admit to herself that even she hadn't had this much fun in, well, in more time than she cared to think about. And she hadn't felt this happy in years, either. Hank was spoiling both of them. If only nothing would come along to spoil it. She hadn't heard a thing from Jeffrey and suspected Vicky had been mistaken. Either that, or Jeffrey had only been in town for a quick visit, then had left. "Want to go feed the ducks again?" Hank asked, craning his neck to look up at the four-year-old.

"Can't," Amanda replied, her sunny smile dimming. "No mowe ducky food."

Hank slid her to the ground and fished in his pocket. "If I give you another quarter, can you get it out of the machine by yourself?"

Her smile immediately brightened and she bobbed her head up and down. After taking the quarter from him, she took a few steps in the direction of the vending machines, then stopped and turned around. "Thank you."

Hank's dimpled grin appeared. "You're welcome."

"You're spoiling her rotten," Lizzie told him when her daughter was out of earshot.

He shrugged. "Every kid should be spoiled now and then."

Together, they walked across the grass and found an empty bench near the duck pond. "When Amanda does things with Vicky and Dean and the boys, she's just one of the crowd. You treat her as if she's special. It makes all the difference in a day like today."

After checking on Amanda, who had retrieved the food and was heading for a group of waddling ducks, Hank settled on the bench next to Lizzie. "She is special."

"I've always thought so, but then I'm prejudiced." Lizzie leaned back, letting the sun warm her face. "I try to spend as much time as I can with her, but it's never as much or as often as I'd like. I'm always afraid I'm depriving her of something. That she'll grow up with a chip on her shoulder because I couldn't give her more time and attention."

"You don't give yourself enough credit."

Lizzie shook her head and closed her eyes. "That's pretty hard to do."

The next thing she knew Hank was pulling her up. With one arm around her, he turned her so she could see her daughter. "Look at her. Does she look like an unhappy child to you?" he asked, his voice soft but demanding.

Amanda knelt on the ground near a group of ducks, who were busy picking at the feed she'd scattered in front of them. Even at a distance, Lizzie could hear her giggles. "No. She looks like a very happy little girl, without a care in the world." She turned to look at him. "Thank you."

Their gazes held for a moment, until Hank smiled and withdrew his arm to drape it along the back of the bench behind her, once they'd sat down again. "Hey, I'm having a good time, too."

For once, Lizzie didn't want him to pull away. This was too nice and she was feeling happier than ever. Instead of keeping the small distance between them, she moved closer to him. "So am I."

He looked at her and his brown eyes darkened. "I can die a happy man."

His voice held a decided husky note, sending tiny flames skipping along her nerves. "I certainly hope not."

As if a traffic light had turned green, Hank brushed her shoulder with the tips of his fingers. "Not what? Die? Or shouldn't I be happy?"

His rough fingers trailing across her bare skin felt delicious, and Lizzie wished that just this once she could let herself go. She longed to be held again, the way he had that night in her office. She wanted to feel his strong arms around her, to press her palms against the solid wall of his chest. If only she could do that without the guilt of her past barging into her thoughts.

"Of course you should be happy," she managed to say. "Everyone should be."

He moved closer. "I know what would make me even happier."

"What?"

One corner of his mouth quirked up at the corner. "This."

It wasn't much of a warning to the soft kiss he placed on her lips. Before she knew it, the kiss was over. She wondered if she had imagined it, but the kiss, as gentle as butterfly wings, had left her lips tingling and wanting more.

"Hank—"

"Shh," he whispered, pressing his finger against her lips. "Don't tell me I shouldn't have done that."

Telling him "no" was the last thing on her mind. "I wasn't going to."

One dark eyebrow raised, then he leaned back. "I've been thinking about Daniel this week."

Lizzie held her breath. He hadn't been willing to discuss his grandfather with her. And she hadn't wanted to ask. He had clearly kept her out of it.

"Don't worry, Lizzie. I've been fair."

She offered him a smile. "I never thought you wouldn't be, when it came down to it."

"It's just that—well, you had to know my mom," he went on, hesitantly. "We never had much. But we never went without, either. Finding out where she came from was a shock. That girl in the picture looked like her, but it wasn't her. I just kept thinking that if he had taken the time to get to know my dad, a lot of things would've been different."

Lizzie thought of the things Hank had told her about his childhood. "But you were happy growing up, weren't you?"

"Yeah. But now I wonder if my mom was." He stood and stuffed his hands in the pockets of his jeans. Pacing in front of the bench, he went on. "I just keep wondering why she didn't tell me about Daniel."

"Hank, you were only a little boy," she pointed out.

He stopped in front of her. "But she lied to me. Outright lied. And if Daniel really did try to contact her—if she returned his letters unopened—" He shook his head. "I told him my parents weren't proud, but I'm beginning to wonder if I was wrong. If I was, I'd be crazy to stay with Crown."

Fear sent a chill through Lizzie. In the distance, she heard the ducks' quacking and Amanda's shrieks of delight, but all she could think about was that Hank might be leaving. Soon. "What do you mean?"

Sighing, he sank to the bench beside her. Leaning his elbows on his knees, he clasped his hands and stared at the duck pond. "Did pride keep her away, or was it because she hated what he represented?"

With her heart pounding, Lizzie tried to answer. "That's something you'll probably never know." She thought about how his mother must have felt when her father wouldn't accept the young man she loved. "She was young, Hank. It's easy to make poor choices. Maybe it was pride. But the past isn't as important as how you feel about your relationship with Daniel. Do you like him as a person?"

"He's a fair man," he admitted. "He treats his employees with respect."

"Are you happy working for him?"

He smiled and turned to her. "I hate to say it, but yeah, I do. I even like my job in the office. It isn't the same as being out on the site, but it isn't as bad as I thought it would be."

The announcement came as a surprise and Lizzie's heart soared. Maybe Hank would stay for a while, after all. "Then that's what's important."

"But knowing he's my grandfather—that I'm a part of this huge conglomerate—keeps getting in the way." Standing again, he took her hand. "Come on. Let's get Amanda and find the lions before we head home."

Lizzie wasn't sure she wanted the conversation to end, but she knew that Hank was going to have to work things out on his own. She had said all she could.

"One more thing," Hank said as they approached Amanda. "Would you have dinner with me tomorrow night?"

Smiling, she gave him the only answer she could. "I'd love to."

His answering grin produced his dimples. "Good. Vicky already said she'd watch Amanda."

Lizzie stared at him. "You said something to my sister?"

"I didn't want you to have any excuses." Before she could answer, they reached Amanda, who had run out of duck food and stood watching the birds as they swam in the pond. "Let's go, cookie," he told her daughter.

Amanda took his hand and looked up at him. "Are we leaving?"

"Not yet, but soon."

With one hand free, Amanda took Lizzie's hand, and they walked toward the concrete pathway, Amanda in the middle, swinging their hands and laughing. "We're just like a family," she said.

The innocent comment brought Lizzie to a halt. Could she handle Amanda's broken heart, and her own, when the time came? She prayed she would and even let herself pray that the time would never come. Instead of revealing her panic, she said nothing.

"Come on, Mommy," Amanda cried, tugging on Lizzie's hand.

Over the top of her head, Hank gave Lizzie a look she couldn't identify. A voice in her head told her she was getting in too deep, but it was too late. She was already falling in love with Hank.

"Are you going to tell me what's going on?" Lizzie asked when Hank parked his rental car in front of the fashionable boutique. He grinned and shook his head, knowing Lizzie well enough to know she would refuse to go along with his plan if he told her.

He had done a little investigating and learned that, although Images, Inc., appeared to be a prosperous business, Lizzie was struggling to make ends meet; she had nearly lost it by using the money she had saved to help pay her mother's medical bills. That, coupled with the fact that Vicky had let it slip that it was Lizzie's birthday and she'd offered to watch Amanda, had given him an idea. He had stopped at her office and insisted she come with him, refusing to explain why.

"I thought we'd do some shopping," he answered, getting out of the car.

She waited until he circled the car and opened the door for her. "What are we shopping for?"

"Tonight."

With one foot on the sidewalk and the rest of her still in the car, she stopped and stared at him. "Tonight?"

He grinned as he helped her out of the car and steered her toward the shop. "You'll see."

"Miss Edwards!" the silver-haired saleswoman greeted Lizzie. "How nice to see you. Is there something special I can help you with today?"

Before Lizzie had a chance to say a word, Hank answered for her. "Miss Edwards is looking for a dress."

Lizzie spun around and stared at him.

"Lizzie, sweetheart, close your mouth," he whispered to her. "It isn't ladylike to gape."

She immediately snapped her mouth shut, but continued to stare at him. "What do you think you're doing?" she asked in a whisper.

"Shopping," he told her and quickly turned to her favorite salesclerk. "We're looking for a dress for her to wear to dinner tonight. A very special dinner."

The woman's eyebrows raised and she smiled. "*Ooooh*, wonderful. We've just received a new shipment, and I thought of Miss Edwards the moment I saw them."

"Then lead the way, Mrs....?"

"Sanders," she answered with a charming smile. "Roberta Sanders."

Hank ignored Lizzie's narrowed eyes. Her threatening expression wasn't going to stop him.

As Mrs. Sanders led them to a section at the rear of the store, Lizzie pulled on his shirtsleeve. "Hank!" she whispered.

"Hmm?" he answered, pretending his attention was on their clerk.

"What are you doing?" Lizzie demanded.

"Getting you a new dress," he whispered out of the side of his mouth before flashing Mrs. Sanders a grin and nodding at whatever it was she was saying.

"Whatever for? I have dresses."

He looked down at her. "Not like what I'm looking for, I'll bet."

"What—"

"Here we are," Mrs. Sanders sang out, cutting off Lizzie's question. Stopping at a rack, the salesclerk went directly to Lizzie's size and flipped through the rainbow of dresses. She pulled out two.

He took one look and shook his head. "No, that's not what I had in mind. They're nice dresses, but I was thinking of something a little more..." He leaned down closer to Mrs. Sanders, but made sure Lizzie could still hear every word he said. "...feminine. Even...sexy. Miss Edwards is a beautiful woman—"

"Oh, I couldn't agree more!" Mrs. Sanders interrupted. "Why, her coloring is simply stunning, and her figure is...well, let's just say it's been many years since I've had a figure even close to what she has and, even now, I don't see many like hers."

"Then you understand," Hank said, straightening, and flashed her another smile. "Why don't I just look around on my own?"

"Oh, yes, please," Mrs. Sanders agreed, stepping aside.

Lizzie watched in silence as he went from rack to rack, looking for the perfect dress. He finally found a black dress he thought would be perfect for her. Not that he had a clue about women's clothing, but he liked the way the front of it dipped and the bottom curled up on the edges.

He pulled it out and held it out to her. She gasped, and the look on her face caused him to smile. "Not bad, huh?" he asked. "Why don't you try it on?"

She took it from him and managed a smile. "Hank," she began once again, "this dress is— Well, the neckline is—"

"You have great taste, Lizzie, but this time I want to give it a try." With his hand at her back, he guided her to the dressing room where Mrs. Sanders pointed. "If you need any help with the zipper, Lizzie, you just give a shout."

"Hank—"

"Mrs. Sanders will be happy to help, I'm sure."

Lizzie gave the salesclerk a wobbly smile and disappeared into the dressing room.

Hank waited. And waited. What was taking so long? "Lizzie?"

"I'll be right out," she called.

When she walked out of the dressing room, his mouth went dry.

"Oh, Miss Edwards!" Mrs. Sanders cried. "You look like a dream." She turned to Hank. "Doesn't she?"

He nodded and stared at her, unable to do anything else.

"Hank?"

He tried to speak. "Lizzie." The name sounded like a croak. He cleared his throat. "Lizzie, it's perfect."

Her smile was brilliant. "I hate to say it, but I think so, too, although I've never had anything like it."

Mrs. Sanders bustled over. "Let me help you slip out of it, then I'll ring it up and wrap it for you so it doesn't get crushed." She looked over her shoulder at Hank. "You do want the dress, right?"

"By all means," he replied. "And without an argument," he told Lizzie.

"I really can't let you pay—"

"I brought you in here and I chose the dress. I'll take care of it, and that's that. Besides, it's a birthday present from Amanda and me."

Her mouth dropped opened. "She told you?"

He shook his head. "Nope. She never said a word."

For a second, her eyes narrowed, then she smiled. "I'll have to remember to thank Vicky."

As Mrs. Sanders followed her into the dressing room, he could hear the older woman chattering on and on. "That's some man out there," she said as they disappeared.

Hank didn't catch Lizzie's reply, but he hoped it was complimentary.

Lizzie watched Amanda join her cousins in front of the television. "Thanks for watching Amanda tonight," she told her sister.

"You deserve a little happiness," Vicky said, then turned quickly and walked into the kitchen. But not before Lizzie noticed her sister's reddened eyes.

"Vicky?" she asked, following her. "What's wrong?"

Shaking her head, Vicky sniffed. "Nothing."

Lizzie knew her sister too well to let her get away with the remark. Taking her by the shoulders, she sat Vicky down in a chair at the table, then took a seat in the one next to her.

Vicky waved a dismissing hand at her, while her eyes filled with tears. "Hank will be here any minute. You go have a good time."

Lizzie's concern mounted. It wasn't like Vicky to cry. Something serious must be wrong. "How can I have a good time if I'm worried about you all night? Is it Mom?"

Shaking her head, Vicky swiped at a stray tear. "Mom is fine. Everybody is fine. Except..."

Lizzie reached to pull a tissue from the box in the center of the table, then handed it to her sister. "Except what?"

With a weak smile, Vicky took the tissue and dabbed at her eyes. Taking a deep, wobbly breath, she dropped her hands to her lap, twisting the tissue in her fingers. "Dean had an affair."

Lizzie's heart jumped to her throat. Shocked, she sat silent for a moment, unable to utter a word. It didn't make sense. "Dean?" She shook her head. "I don't believe it."

"Why not?"

"For one thing, he loves you to distraction, and for another, he's the perfect family man."

"Things aren't always as they seem, Lizzie."

She knew that was true. But Dean? It wasn't possible. Vicky and Dean had been the perfect couple since they'd begun dating in high school. He had attended college in Lawrence, Kansas, so he would be close to her. They waited to marry until they were able to afford the perfect place to live. He had done well at his job, already stepping into a top position in an electronics company. He had always loved Vicky, and he *was* the perfect family man. Lizzie had never expected less. Vicky had always been the perfect daughter of the two of them. Nothing short of the perfect marriage, the perfect family, for Vicky. Lizzie had envied her since they were children. Dean couldn't possibly have had an affair.

"You're sure about this?" she asked, still not believing it could be true.

Vicky nodded. "Very sure. He admitted it to me. Yesterday. That's why we didn't go to the zoo."

"What are you going to do?"

"I was going to see an attorney," Vicky said, "but there's a...well, there's a small problem with that." Before Lizzie could ask what it was, Vicky hurried on. "He begged me to get counseling with him."

Relieved that someone was being at least a little sensible, Lizzie searched her mind for something to say. "Many couples survive a spouse's straying. Counseling will help. It's a very good sign that he suggested it."

Vicky nodded, then blew her nose. "He said he realizes he was wrong." She looked at her sister. "He said he's sorry, and I truly think he is, but..."

"But it's hard to trust," Lizzie finished for her. "If he feels that way and is truly sorry, and if he's willing to go to counseling, the trust will return."

Vicky dabbed at her eyes again. "I'm sure that's true, but it isn't the problem."

Lizzie could only think of one thing. "You don't want a divorce, do you?"

"Of course I don't! But that may be what happens anyway." She folded her hands in her lap, the damp, crumpled tissue clasped tightly between them, then she looked Lizzie in the eye. "I'm pregnant."

Knowing her sister and brother-in-law had stopped at what they had said many times was the perfect number of children, Lizzie was more than surprised. "But that's wonderful!"

Vicky gave her a watery smile. "It would be, but Dean doesn't want any more children. I think that's what led to his wandering. We argued and argued about it. I've been so jealous of you, Lizzie. You and Amanda. I've wanted a little girl of my own for so long. And I'm going to have one. I just know it. But she may not have a daddy, when Dean finds out."

"Jealous? Of me?" Lizzie felt as if she had been hit with a sledgehammer, but she managed to stand and put her arms around her older sister. "Oh, Vicky, I've felt the same about you for so very long. But I'm sure Dean won't be angry about a baby. Not once he really thinks about it."

"Aunt Lizzie, Hank is here," Denny called from the family room.

Vicky pulled away from Lizzie's embrace. "Go. Hank's waiting."

"Hank will understand," Lizzie told her, not wanting to leave her in such an emotional state.

Getting to her feet, Vicky straightened her shirt and put on the worst imitation of a smile Lizzie had ever seen. "I'll be fine. It's mostly the hormones." Turning Lizzie around, she placed her hands on Lizzie's shoulders and gave her a push in the direction of the door. "Listen to your big sister. Go to dinner with Hank and have a wonderful time. I'll deal with my problems."

"We'll talk later," Lizzie promised as the doorbell chimed.

By the time they reached the door, all three children were gathered around Hank. "Leave Hank alone so he can take Aunt Lizzie to dinner," Vicky told the noisy group.

Hank looked up from his admirers and gave a low whistle. "That's some dress, Miss Edwards. Whoever picked that out has great taste."

In spite of the worry over her sister and the way her head was reeling from learning she had been wrong about nearly everything in her life, Lizzie laughed. "You *would* say that."

When the cousins had finally drifted back to the television, Lizzie gave her sister a hug. "We *will* talk later. That's a promise."

"It sounds more like a threat," Vicky said with a weak smile. "I'll be fine. I have some great plans for the kids tonight." She turned to Hank. "Lizzie doesn't have a curfew, so keep her out as long as you like. Amanda is spending the night with us," she added with a sly smile.

By the look on his face, Hank was obviously stunned by the suggestion. Embarrassed, Lizzie quickly said goodbye and hustled him out the door. "I swear. My sister can get the strangest ideas in her head."

"Is Vicky sick?" Hank asked as they reached his car. "She doesn't look good."

Lizzie would have given anything to dump her concerns about her sister on Hank, but she didn't feel she should. It was family business, and Hank wasn't family, no matter how much the Edwards clan liked him.

As she climbed in the car, it hit her again that Vicky didn't have the fairy-tale life Lizzie had always thought she had. As Vicky had said, things weren't always as they seemed.

"If she's sick, maybe Amanda shouldn't stay with her," Hank said, climbing into the car on the driver's side.

"She isn't sick," Lizzie answered. *Just heartsick.* "Amanda will be fine." But would Vicky? And would Lizzie, after finding out that her ideal couple was more human than she ever would have imagined? No, things weren't always as they seemed. Not at all.

In the darkening interior of the car, she glanced at Hank. It didn't surprise her that he looked great. That much was a given, whether he was in a tuxedo, a workshirt and jeans, or in the well-tailored suit he had chosen for the evening. He looked comfortable. And happy. The last thing she wanted to see was him worrying over her family. And she knew he would if he found out about Dean and Vicky's troubles. He was that kind of man. She wouldn't tell him, but she would think about talking to Dean before she talked with her sister again. She just wasn't sure what she would say. She would ask Hank, but she felt certain he would ask questions she couldn't answer. Somehow, she would think of something. Considering how much her sister had stood beside her, as their parents had, Lizzie couldn't turn her back and do nothing. Maybe someday Hank would understand what "family" meant. But first, she needed to get used to this idea that her sister wasn't perfect. And that would be a big job.

Chapter Eight

"Did I pick the wrong restaurant?" Hank asked, after they had shared what he had hoped would be a perfect evening.

Lizzie turned in the seat to look at him. "I'm sorry. What did you say?"

Sighing, he shook his head. "Maybe you should have a course on dating etiquette at Images, Inc."

"Why? You don't have a problem with that."

"That's good to know. But if it's true, why haven't you said more than a dozen words all evening?"

She opened her mouth as if to answer, but closed it and shook her head. "Nothing important."

The traffic was too heavy to do more than glance at her. He had spent the evening across the table from her, but there had been times when he might as well have been alone. Her mind had been a million miles away.

Instead of turning in the direction he needed to go to take her back to her sister's to pick up Amanda, he kept going. Whatever was bothering her, he had a right to know after spending two hours with her uttering very little more than monosyllabic answers to his questions.

"Where are we going?" she asked, sitting up to look out the windows.

"Oh, you mean you noticed?"

Slumping back in the seat, she sighed. "I'm sorry. I truly am. It's just..."

The second shake of her head made him even more determined to get to the bottom of whatever it was. "I'm taking you to my place." Before she could argue, he held up his hand to stop her. "Vicky said— No. If I remember correctly, she *insisted* that I not bring you home early. Besides, I have coffee. Strong coffee."

"I'd like that."

He took his attention off the road long enough to flash her a smile. "That's the most sensible thing I've heard you say all night."

Minutes later, Hank pulled the car into his parking space in front of the apartment building and turned off the engine. As he got out and circled to open her door, he wondered what it would take to get her to let down her guard. She had done her damnedest to keep him at a distance. What was it about him that scared her off? Before the evening was over, he intended to learn at least that much.

Lizzie hesitated when he held out his hand to help her from the car, then she offered him a warm smile and took his hand. "How do you like the apartment, now that you've lived in it for a while?" she asked as they walked together to the building.

"It's okay. Big, but I'm getting used to it."

Inside, they rode the elevator to his floor in silence. Lizzie seemed lost in thought, as she had all evening since he had picked her up at her sister's house. He had never seen her this quiet. Usually she had something to say, even if it was nothing more than to argue with him. He was getting worried.

At his apartment, he unlocked the door, then opened it and ushered her inside. For an instant, he almost stopped her from entering. He couldn't remember how messy he had left the place. Then he remembered picking up after himself before leaving for the evening and shoving the few dishes he had in the dishwasher, just in case. Nobody had ever called him a slob, but he wasn't Mr. Clean, either. Now that he thought about it, none of that had ever bothered him. Why did it now?

"Make yourself at home," he said, pointing to the oversize sofa. "I'll get the coffee started." He headed for the kitchen, then stopped and turned. "Or would you rather have something else?"

Barely settled on the sofa, she looked at him. "Something else?"

"Yeah." He shifted from one foot to the other, not sure what the hell had made him ask that. "You know. A glass of wine. A beer. Maybe a martini?" He didn't know if he had all the necessary ingredients to make a martini, but if that's what she wanted, he would find a way to do it.

She scrunched up her face. "White wine," she said, considering the offer. "That sounds good. Do you have some?"

Hank smiled at his stroke of good luck. The previous occupant of the apartment had left behind a bottle in the refrigerator. "White wine coming right up."

In the kitchen, he poured her drink, then grabbed a beer for himself and poured it into a glass so he wouldn't look like a hick. After all, this was the woman who had refined him into the almost-*GQ* guy that he was now.

With drinks in hand, he returned to the living room to find her standing at the picture window with her arms wrapped around her waist, staring out into the darkness. "Lizzie?"

Obviously startled, she turned, and he recognized the worry and concern in her eyes. She quickly hid it with a smile. "It's not a bad view."

He set their drinks on the glass-topped coffee table and joined her at the window. The urge to slip his arms around her was strong, but he clasped his hands behind his back to keep from acting on it. Until she gave him some kind of sign that she would welcome his touch, he would keep his hands to himself. She had taught him how important it was to be a gentleman and, by damn, he would act like one.

He stood that way for what seemed like an eternity, watching her reflection in the glass, until he couldn't stand it any longer. "You wanna talk about it?"

Her gaze met his in the image reflected before them, but she didn't answer.

"I'm a good listener. Seems like that's what I've done my whole life."

To his surprise, she turned and moved closer to lean her head against his chest.

He wasn't sure if this was the sign he was looking for or not. And he sure as hell didn't want to make the wrong move and scare her off. Being careful not to do exactly that, he slipped an arm around her. It wasn't quite what he had in mind, but it would have to do.

Her sigh was soft, but the tension in her body was even more noticeable. "I don't know where to start."

Counseling wasn't his strong suit, but he had always done well in psychology class. He at least had a grasp of it, especially after the many nights he'd spent in bars and taverns, listening to others tell of their troubles. His stint as a bartender in Yuma, Arizona, had merely affirmed his suspicions. All most people needed was someone to talk to.

"The first thing we do is get you comfortable," he said and steered her to the sofa. She didn't argue, which he considered a good sign. Once he had her settled, he handed her the glass of wine.

"Is it okay if I take my shoes off?" she asked, taking the drink from him.

"Sure. You can take off your shoes. Whatever is comfortable." Glancing around the room, he spied the pillows he had tossed on a chair earlier in the day. "How about a pillow?"

Her smile was grateful but strained. "Thank you." She took a sip of wine, then leaned her head back and closed her eyes.

Grabbing two pillows, he settled next to her, but not too close. She took the pillow and he waited for her to say something, but she didn't. His only option was to ask. "What happened?"

A ghost of a smile appeared on her face. Opening her eyes only a little, she gave him a long, lazy sideways glance. "Lots. You can't imagine."

But the smile quickly disappeared and she closed her eyes again, leaving him to wonder what caused it. Listening to guys in a bar who had had too many drinks was easy. It only required paying attention, nodding or shaking his head now and then, and asking the right questions. But with a woman like Lizzie? He was at a loss as to what to ask.

Before he could think of a good question, she let out a long, sad sigh. "Sometimes I envy you not having a family."

The statement took him by surprise and he stared at her. "Why?"

She moved, as if getting comfortable, balancing the wineglass in one hand, but she still didn't look all that at ease. "Because if you did something wrong and hurt people, you didn't spend the rest of your life trying to make up for it."

Lizzie do something wrong? He couldn't believe it. She was so perfect. So precise in everything. And so damned uptight. Her statement proved it. "What do you think you did?"

Opening her eyes, she sat up and turned to look at him, drawing one shapely leg onto the sofa. "It's not that I 'think' I did something wrong. I know I did."

"And what was that?"

She blinked her wide, disbelieving eyes, not once, but twice. "I'm sure you can guess, Hank."

He shook his head. "Unless you're talking about Amanda—and I don't see how that's bad—I can't think of anything. Did you rob a bank? Shoot somebody?"

Shoulders drooping, her chin dropped. "No."

"Embezzle a company? Break up a marriage?"

At the last question, she shot him a slow look. "No."

"Then what?"

Her head moved from side to side, and she let out another sigh. "I hurt my family. I caused them shame."

"Sounds to me like you're the one who's ashamed, and I sure can't see why."

"You don't know what I was like."

"You don't know what I was like, either," he replied. When she didn't respond, he went on. "What difference does it make what people were like when they were kids? Isn't it what they've made of themselves as adults that's important?"

"I suppose."

This wasn't the Lizzie he knew. His Lizzie had a spark of fire. She knew what she wanted and she got it, but she didn't run over people in the process. She was kind, she was gentle, but he had seen a strength in her, too. That was what had drawn him to her. And it was what kept him in Kansas City. Not the job with Crown. Not having found a member of his family. It was Lizzie.

Shocked at his own private admission, he suddenly got to his feet.

"Where are you going?" she asked.

He wondered the same thing. All he knew was that he had to get away, before he did something he might regret. "I'm just going to go make us that coffee."

But making coffee was only an excuse. If he wasn't careful, he would care too much to leave when the time came. And the time would come. Wouldn't it?

He wanted nothing more than to take her in his arms and show her how special she was. But he had a feeling that doing it wouldn't help her. He shouldn't get involved. He was in too deep as it was. But he couldn't stop himself. Whatever was eating at her, it went deep. It was time she opened up the wounds to cleanse them. She had so much love to give, but she refused to give it to anyone but her family. Whether he stayed in Kansas City or not, the least he could do was to help her.

And he wouldn't do it the way his body cried out to.

Lizzie leaned back against the sofa, afraid of what had to be done next. She couldn't bear to tell Hank the things she knew she needed to. What would he think of her? He already knew about the mistake she had made when she was young and accepted it much better than most people did, without questions. But what he didn't know was what had led her to make it. After talking to Vicky, it was the most damning of all. She was an even bigger fool than she had ever imagined.

Hank came back into the room carrying two steaming mugs. "I hope it isn't too strong for you."

"It'll be fine," she said, taking the cup he offered. Instead of taking a sip, she put the mug on the table next to her wineglass. "I'm sorry about tonight. I didn't mean to spoil our dinner."

He chose to sit on the sofa, but not near her, and she felt even worse for the way she had acted throughout the evening. It wasn't like her. But after thinking over what Vicky had told her and what it revealed about so many things, she wasn't sure she would ever be the same again.

"I'm more concerned about you than a dinner," he said.

Nodding, she took a deep breath. It was now or never. "I'm worried about Vicky."

"Is something wrong with her?" The concern in his voice nearly brought tears to her eyes. Why should he care?

"Yes. No. Oh, it's such a mess. I'm such a mess," she blurted.

"You?" His laughter rumbled deep in his chest. "Lady, I've never known anyone more well put together than you. And I don't mean just that body of yours."

The heat of a blush warmed her face and she shook her head. "I thought I had a handle on things. I thought I understood everything. But...well, everything has changed. Nothing is as I thought it was."

"What do you mean by everything?"

She couldn't risk looking at him for fear she couldn't continue. "My life." For a moment, she couldn't speak, but she finally forced the words out. "All my life, I've thought Vicky was perfect. She was our parents' favorite. Smart, pretty, popular in school. Perfect. She never caused anyone a moment of worry."

"And you know that for a fact?"

"At least not that I know of," she admitted. "But today was a revelation of sorts. I found out things I'm not sure I wanted to know. Or maybe I did, secretly, but they're just so...I don't know. I guess it's just that I learned that appearances can be deceiving."

"What happened?" he asked, when she didn't continue.

She shook her head, still mystified by it all. "I learned my sister isn't perfect."

"That doesn't surprise me."

"I learned that her marriage isn't perfect," she admitted, not wanting to go into the details.

"That doesn't surprise me, either. From what I've seen, nobody's is. Maybe that's what keeps it interesting. For some."

She didn't fail to notice his last words and what they meant. Once again, Hank had made it clear that he wasn't a marrying man. But that was okay, wasn't it?

Standing, she crossed to the window, but instead of admiring the view, she paced and talked, unable to stop herself, now that she had started. "I've lived my whole life wanting to be like my sister. Perfect. But I messed that up because of the very same reasons. It was because of my perception of her that I did the things I did." She stopped and shook her head, not yet understanding what it all meant. "I thought Jeffrey was the answer and found that, not only wasn't he, but it made things even worse. I've borne the shame of that." She turned to look at Hank. "But through all of it, Vicky was there for me. My parents were, too, even though I didn't see it. And Hank, she told me she envied me. Can you believe it? Vicky envies *me*."

"Doesn't surprise me."

Still unable to make sense of it, she returned to the sofa and sat beside him. With only a few words from him, and a lot of her own rambling, she felt better than she had since Vicky had dropped the bomb about her marriage and pregnancy.

"You're something else, Hank Davis," she said, sliding closer to plant a kiss on his cheek. But when he pulled away, she was surprised. "I—I'm sorry, I guess I shouldn't have done that."

Hurt and not wanting him to notice, she got to her feet. She hadn't thought what he might think of her.

Now she could add foolish to her list of woes. Spying her glass of wine on the table, she picked it up and drained it, then turned to look at him.

"Maybe I should take you home," he said and made a move to stand.

Whether it was the wine that suddenly made her light-headed and her heart pound, she wasn't sure. But she knew she didn't want to go. She couldn't let him take her home and then just walk away. And that's what he intended to do. He had that scared-as-a-rabbit-and-wanting-to-run look. She had seen that same look in the mirror five years ago, when she learned she was pregnant with Amanda. Jeffrey had worn the same expression when he walked out on her.

Closing her eyes, she silently prayed for an answer.

"Lizzie?"

She shook her head, not wanting to see that guarded look in his eyes. "No. Not yet. I—" She shook her head again, then prepared herself to face him. When she did, the look on his face wasn't that of someone who wanted his space. It was complete capitulation, and she felt the same. Why else would she still be there, ready to beg him to hold her?

She didn't have to beg. Without warning, he pulled her onto his lap, tilted her chin and claimed her lips. She didn't try to stop him. She didn't even hesitate. Since the kiss they had shared at the zoo, she had wanted this. And more. Her good sense had kept her from taking action. But she no longer cared about good sense. Not with his mouth demanding more and more of her. Not with his hands gliding the length of her. This time she pushed the warning voice from her mind. She would enjoy this, wherever it might take her. She had been good for so long. So very long. She deserved to celebrate her womanhood.

With his hands and his mouth, he made her feel cherished. Gentle one minute, demanding the next, she matched her pace with his, as if it were second nature to be this way with this man. When he started to end the kiss and ease away, she pulled him back again. It wasn't something as simple as wanting him. She needed this for sheer survival. She needed *him*.

Her pulse raced, her heart pounded. Blood, heated to the boiling point, ebbed and flowed to places she had all but forgotten. She heard his groan, knew this might be the only time this would ever happen and gave herself up completely to his kiss.

Hank knew he needed to gain control, but kissing Lizzie was like a drug he couldn't give up. He had been fighting it since the first time, in her office. He had suspected she wasn't as polished and prim as she appeared. But suspecting it hadn't been enough for him. He'd had to prove it to himself.

Twisting, he moved to ease her down on the sofa and stretch out next to her. Pulling her even closer, he reveled in the way her body molded to his and suddenly knew what heaven must be like. He deepened the kiss, tasting and teasing, and still wasn't satisfied. Reaching up, he pulled the confining pins from her hair, then tangled his fingers in the silky strands. He had been dreaming of doing it since the first moment he had laid eyes on her.

She was so close, he felt the heat of her body and wondered if they would melt into each other. He'd never felt so hot a fire for a woman. He wanted her, all of her, and for an instant was ready to have her. Until he realized what that might do to her.

Reluctantly slowing the kiss to finally end it with a brush of his lips against hers because he couldn't stand the thought of losing contact with her, he whispered. "Lizzie…"

The only answer from her was a moan.

He gently grasped her hands from around his neck and slowly pulled them away. His breathing was labored, but he managed to speak. "I—well, I shouldn't have done that. But, dammit, I wanted to."

"And I wanted you to," she said, her breathing as ragged as his.

Slowly he nodded. "Yeah. But before this goes any further…"

"It's okay," she said and slipped one hand from his. Reaching up, she curled her fingers at the back of his neck to pull him to her for another kiss. "I'm an adult. I know what I'm doing."

He placed his hand on hers and kissed her gently, then helped her to a sitting position beside him. "I don't want you leaving here with regrets."

"I wouldn't—"

"You might. I might. And I don't want that to happen."

She stared at him. "You might regret it?" Pain shimmered in her eyes. Shaking her head, she pulled away and stood. "You know, you're right."

When she started to turn away, he got up from the sofa and grabbed her hand before she could move. "That's not what I meant. I just don't want something to happen too soon. I know people do it all the time, but this isn't our time. Not yet."

Our time. The words made him stop and think.

Rushing into something before they were ready—really ready, in a way that wasn't something more than two people caught up in the passion of the moment—would be foolish. Very foolish. He wished he could make her understand that he was doing it for her, not himself. If he had his way... He could tell by the depth of emotion in her eyes that if he hadn't stopped, there would have been no going back. He couldn't let that happen. It could very well put an end to everything.

Lifting her hand, he pressed her palm to his lips. "There will be another time. I promise you that."

Her gaze met his, and he recognized the hint of regret he saw there. But even more, he saw relief and gratitude. It made him glad that he had gained control before it was too late.

She looked away, as if she was afraid of what he might see. "I'll just go fix my hair," she said, turning toward the bathroom.

Unable to resist touching the flaming waves that spilled over her shoulders, he pulled her back and dipped his hand into her hair again. "Why don't you leave it down? I like it this way." His gravelly voice didn't surprise him. He might have stopped the kisses, but he couldn't stop wanting her.

"Maybe someday," she said with a sad smile.

He released her and watched her walk away. He could only hope he hadn't caused more damage by calling a halt to things than he would have if he hadn't. He couldn't have done it for anyone else. Only Lizzie. And he couldn't promise he could ever do it again.

Shoving a hand through his hair, he knew he was going to have to make a decision. Soon. Should he stay in Kansas City and try to build something with Lizzie? Or should he leave, before it was too late? If he didn't plan to stay, he couldn't lead her on any longer. He cared about her. Too much. And it scared him to think he might be falling in love with her.

Lizzie returned before he had a chance to think about the possibilities. With a hesitant smile, she picked up her purse, then came to stop in front of him. Standing on her tiptoes, she kissed the corner of his mouth. "Thank you."

The kiss took him by surprise, but her words stunned him. "For what?"

"For being you." She turned and walked away, stopping when she reached the door. "I think I should go home now."

"Yeah," he said, agreeing without thinking. He wondered what she had meant. Shaking his head to clear it, he grabbed his keys from the coffee table where he had tossed them and joined her at the door. "Yeah," he repeated, even though letting her go was the last thing he wanted to do.

Hank looked up from his desk to see Daniel enter his office. Putting his work aside, he stood.

"Sit down, Hank," Daniel told him with a wave of his hand. "There's no reason for us to stand on ceremony with each other. We're family."

The words sounded strange to Hank, but not unwelcome. Daniel Wallace—his grandfather—had done enough penance. Hank had seen what guilt had done to Lizzie and suspected it had done the same to Daniel. It wasn't something he wanted to perpetuate. The man had paid a high price. So had Hank's mother. He had come to understand that he had made his mother a saint in his mind. But she was human. Both she and Daniel had made a mistake. A mistake born of pride. Hank wouldn't do the same.

"I could've come to your office," Hank told him, as the older man sank onto the chair on the other side of the desk. "All you had to do was call."

Daniel smiled and shook his head. "I like coming in here to see you work. It makes my heart glad."

Hank couldn't help but return the smile. Sitting, he leaned back in his chair and refused to let the what-ifs enter his mind. Since learning about his mother's past, he had spent too much time wondering what might have happened if things had been different. The past was gone. He intended to enjoy the present and look forward to the future, whatever that might be.

"Have you made a decision?" Daniel asked.

Hank nodded. "I'm staying. At least for now. Six months, maybe more."

Daniel closed his eyes. Opening them again, he smiled. "You're getting along well then? You like it here?"

Hank nodded again. "It's not what I'm used to, but I can't say it isn't interesting work. I'm adjusting."

"I would have been surprised if you weren't," Daniel said, pride shining in his eyes.

Hank found that, after getting to know his grandfather, he couldn't dislike him. "You seem to know a lot about people."

"I've had a lot of years to learn," Daniel replied. "And mistakes are always the best teacher. Like the mistakes I made with your mother."

"We all make mistakes."

Sighing, Daniel pressed his hand to his heart. "I

made them out of love. You understand that, don't you?"

Hank thought for a moment. He had no doubt that Daniel had loved his daughter and had only wanted the best for her. "You were trying to protect her. I might have done the same thing."

Daniel said nothing, but seemed to relax, and Hank realized how much he had grown to care for his grandfather. "If things had been different—"

"But they weren't, so we make the best of it."

"The past is behind us," Hank said, nodding. "We make the best of what we can." For a moment he hesitated, not comfortable sharing his feelings. "I'm glad we met," he finally admitted.

"So am I, Hank. So am I."

After a short, easy silence, Daniel put his hands on the arms of the chair, shifted his position, then cleared his throat. "I'm not here for a social visit, although I enjoy those much more. I'm here on business. An offer, to be exact."

"An offer?" As far as Hank was concerned, another offer from Daniel was more than he deserved. He didn't feel he had proven himself in his current job to warrant more. "You don't need—"

Daniel put up his hand, stopping Hank's protest. "It isn't because you need it. It's because I need it."

Hank didn't feel it wise to argue. Nothing he could say would stop his grandfather. The man had gotten his way for too long, and Hank wasn't about to try to change that. If he had learned nothing else since joining Crown and Wallace International, it was that Daniel knew what he was doing.

"It's like this," Daniel continued, although he looked ill at ease, "I'm well past the age of retirement. I could've left everything in the hands of people well qualified to run the whole shebang. But I didn't want to let go of the reins."

Hank wasn't sure what the conversation was leading up to. And he wasn't sure he wanted to know. "So don't," he replied.

Tipping his head back, Daniel laughed. "Don't worry. I'm not senile or crazy enough to just up and leave it. But the time isn't that far away when I won't be able, physically or mentally, to do what needs to be done. What I have in mind is a slow easing out, until I'm sure things are in the right hands."

Hank forced himself to ask the question that had to be asked. "And whose hands are those?"

"I never thought there would be anyone to leave all this to. I knew I had a grandson, but, as time went by, the possibility of ever knowing him grew smaller and smaller. You don't know it, but I may know more about you than even you do. I didn't tell you this, but I've watched you for the past two years. I know the kind of person you are. I think I know the kind of person you will be. I want you to lead Wallace International when I'm gone."

Although he had seen it coming, Hank was overwhelmed by the offer. "I don't—"

"Of course you don't," Daniel interrupted. He levered himself from the chair and stood before Hank's desk.

Hank got to his feet, but couldn't speak. Words were beyond him.

"I'm not asking for an answer now," Daniel continued. "Think about it. Before you decide, we'll talk. There's time, and I don't want you to agree to something you don't understand and truly want."

"Okay." There wasn't much Hank could say, so he reached across the desk.

Daniel took his hand. "No decisions. Just think."

"I will," Hank promised.

He watched Daniel leave the office, then sank to his chair. Head of Wallace International? Him? How had all this happened in such a short span of time? First the offer of the foreman's job, then the move from New Mexico and the life he knew. Then Lizzie.

Lizzie. He needed to call her and tell her the news. He could only imagine what she would say, and he found it impossible not to feel some excitement of his own. Life seemed to be making his decisions for him.

Reaching for the phone, he stopped before touching it. No, he had a better idea. One he had been considering for some time. And he couldn't wait to see her face.

Chapter Nine

Lizzie placed her cup of cold coffee in the office microwave to heat for the second time and tried to focus on what needed to be done before the day was over. Keeping her mind on business hadn't been an easy task for the past few days. Thoughts of Hank and their evening together, as well as her sister's problems, kept creeping in, pushing everything else aside. At least Vicky and Dean were seeing a marriage counselor, but it had taken all Lizzie's concentration just to go through the mail earlier that morning.

"What's that commotion?" she asked, when a loud noise coming from outside the building caught her attention.

"Oh my heavens!" Janine cried from the doorway. "Get out here, Lizzie. You've got to see this."

"See what?" She joined Janine at the open door. Looking outside, her question was answered.

A gleaming black motorcycle sat at the curb, its

engine rumbling. A figure in a black leather jacket bent over it, his face hidden. When he straightened, Lizzie gasped. "Hank!"

Like a small child on Christmas morning, his dimpled grin spread from ear to ear. "How do you like it?" he asked over the noise.

"I think it's loud," she said, raising her voice to be heard above the roar. When his grin turned into a smug smile, she decided not to tell him that it was truly a beautiful machine. "What are you going to do with it?" she asked instead.

"Do? Why I'm going to ride it." He stepped around the bike and took her elbow. "And you're going to ride it with me."

Hank couldn't imagine how badly Lizzie wanted to do just that. Something about the power of the machine made her heart race. But she wasn't going to admit it to him. She knew it was nothing more than another part of her wild side, and he had seen enough of that.

"Well, I'm certainly not riding it now," she forced herself to say.

"Why not? It's a beautiful day, and you don't have a client right now. Come on," he urged, tugging her toward the cycle. "It's the perfect time."

"Hank, look at the way I'm dressed." She gestured toward her sky-blue suit with the straight skirt. But she wanted to ride. Oh, how she wanted to. If only she kept a pair of jeans at the office, but she couldn't climb on behind him dressed as she was.

He released her and climbed on the machine. "Hike up your skirt and climb on. No one will see anything."

She felt her face grow hot and shook her head.

Even if that was true, being that close to him again might not be such a good idea. It was enough just to look at him. He was the quintessential bad boy. All he needed was a lock of stray hair and a pout.

His hair stayed put, but she got the pout. He reached out and took her hand, pulling her closer. With his mouth next to her ear, he said, "I wanted to share this with you."

Her insides melted. How could she tell him no?

Turning, she shrugged, then waved to Janine. "I won't be gone long. Hold down the fort, will you?"

Janine gave a thumbs-up, her grin envious.

Looking around to make certain no one was watching, Lizzie pulled the hem of her skirt as high as she dared. Taking a deep breath of excitement and to ward off the embarrassment of how she must look, she climbed onto the motorcycle behind Hank.

"'Atta girl," he said. "But you'd better scoot up closer and hang on. This thing has power."

She did as she was told, inching as close to him as possible to avoid leaving anything for anyone to see. When he turned his head to grin at her, it was obvious what caught his eye. Her entire leg, pressed against his hip and thigh, was bared for the whole city to see.

His grin widened. "I should've done this sooner."

Even over the noise of the engine, she heard what he said and the husky quality of his voice. Before she could reply, he nudged the accelerator, and they took off. Vowing to never ride with him again, unless she was wearing something more appropriate, she gave in to the inevitable thrill.

She knew she should be worrying about more than her unladylike position. His image was at stake—the image she had worked on for two weeks. But at that moment, she didn't give a fig about images. His or her own.

As they picked up speed, she was more than glad she couldn't see in front of them. The traffic was heavy, but Hank expertly maneuvered the big bike and wove his way out of the heaviest of it. They were soon flying along the expressway, keeping up with the cars on all sides of them.

She forgot about her skirt and enjoyed the sheer exhilaration of the ride. Nothing she could remember doing could beat it. The wind whipped pieces of her hair out of the tight knot and blew long tendrils across her face. As far as she was concerned, this was the closest she had ever come to flying.

Hank angled the cycle toward an exit ramp and slowed their speed. Wanting to ask where they were going, she decided to enjoy the ride and keep quiet. She would know soon enough, since they were now driving through a quiet part of the city.

Slowing even more, he revved the engine, then turned and took a side street, until they came to a small park. Stopping near a picnic table under a group of trees, Hank shut off the motor. "Maybe you'd better get off first," he said.

Grateful that he didn't want to cause her further embarrassment, she slid off with as much grace as she could manage, then tugged her skirt down. "I hate to say it," she told him as he swung his leg and climbed off, "but that was fun. What I want to know is what on earth possessed you to buy a motorcycle?"

He draped his arm around her shoulders and led her toward the picnic table. "It's something I've always wanted, but I never had the means to get one.

Not just money. I had enough. But a bike wasn't practical."

"Thanks for sharing the ride with me."

Settling on the picnic table, he put his arms around her waist and pulled her to stand between his legs. "That isn't all I wanted to share."

It struck her that he wasn't smiling. And he didn't look as if he wanted to kiss her again. What could he want to share? A motorcycle was a sign of independence. At least that's how she had always viewed it. Was his buying it a gesture of what was to come? Was he planning to leave, now that she had let him know that he was something special to her?

"Hey, what's wrong?" He pulled his hand away to gently rub the spot between her eyes. "What's making you frown?"

"What is it you want to share?" she asked, half holding her breath for the worst.

"Daniel made me an offer today."

"Oh?"

He nodded. "Seems he wants me to step into his shoes. Over a period of time, of course."

Surprised and relieved at the same time, Lizzie studied him. She couldn't tell if he was happy or not. "And what did you tell him?"

"Nothing. Yet. He told me to think about it."

Realizing her nerves were causing her to rub her palms along the tops of his thighs, she stopped. "Have you?"

"Some." His gaze traveled past her. "I'm not sure anymore what I want. I thought maybe you and I should talk about it."

Hope fluttered in her heart. This was the first time he had even suggested his stay in Kansas City might be more permanent. And he valued her opinion. Too bad she was beyond being objective about it.

When he looked at her again, his eyes were troubled. "I don't know if I can leave yet," he said, tucking a stray tendril of her hair behind her ear. "I think I want to stay, but…"

If only he hadn't added the *but*, she would have been ecstatic. She had known from the beginning that he had never intended to settle down with her or anyone. He had made that clear, even if he hadn't said it. And she had been all right with that. Still, she had begun to hope.

"You don't have to make a decision right now," she said, her throat feeling tight and achy. "There's plenty of time." Unable to look at him any longer, she glanced down, and the dial of her watch caught her attention. She had an appointment with a new client. Business had picked up in the past two weeks, and she suspected Daniel had something to do with it. "Speaking of time, I'm expecting a prospective client in less than thirty minutes. We'd better get back."

She started to step away from him, but he held her. "Lizzie." When she lifted her head to look at him, he pressed a gentle kiss on her lips. "We can talk about it later."

The ride back to her office wasn't nearly as wild as the ride to the park had been. For one thing, she had sense enough to remove her jacket and cover herself as best as she could. When they pulled up in front of Images, Inc., she was thankful she had. Their arrival on the motorcycle created quite a lot of attention from passers-by.

"I'll talk to you later this evening," Hank said,

sitting astride his bike, while Lizzie gathered her jacket and straightened her clothing. "Maybe we can rent a movie to watch and pop some popcorn."

"I'd like that."

As she bent to kiss his cheek, she heard her name called.

"You haven't changed a bit, have you? Still as wild as ever. Just a few years older."

She turned around at the sound of the familiar voice—a voice she hadn't heard for five years—and her blood turned to ice water in her veins. Hadn't she known this moment would come one day?

"Cat got your tongue?"

"What are you doing here?" she demanded of the man who had left her alone and pregnant with his child.

"I came to see you," he replied, then glanced at Hank. "But I see you're busy, as usual." The smile he offered Hank was almost a leer.

"I am busy," Lizzie said, looking at her watch. "Whether you know it or not, I have a business and an appointment—"

"So your secretary told me."

"Lizzie?" Hank said from behind her.

Turning to look at him, she wasn't sure what to say. Introductions were impossible for her, at the moment. All she wanted to do was get Jeffrey and his smart mouth away from Hank. She had spent five long years growing up and living down the things he knew about her. If he said too much—

"Let's go inside," she told Jeffrey, indicating the door to Images, Inc. "We can talk about whatever it is you want."

"We can talk about my daughter."

Her heart thundered in her chest. *His* daughter? She had plenty to say on that subject. "Yes. Of course we can. But not out here on the sidewalk." Taking a deep breath, she turned to Hank. "I'm sorry, but I have to go do this."

He was staring at Jeffrey and barely looked at her. "Is that Amanda's father?"

"That's right," Jeffrey said. "And I intend to get to know her. And to get to know Lizzie again, too."

Hank's gaze met hers, questions begging to be answered in his eyes.

"Later," she told him, pressing her hand to his cheek. "I promise."

Forcing herself to move, she turned back to Jeffrey. "All right. Let's go inside where you can say whatever it is you seem to need to say."

He followed her to the door and as she went inside, she glanced back, past him, to where Hank still sat on the motorcycle, staring after them. There was nothing she could do, until she talked to Jeffrey. Hank had nothing to worry about. She didn't have any intention of letting Jeffrey back into her life, or of allowing him to have anything to do with Amanda. His name wasn't on the birth certificate. Before he could make any demands, he would have to prove his paternity. And that would take time. As they entered the building, she glanced at him and wondered what she had ever thought was attractive about him.

"Who's he?" Janine whispered as Lizzie passed her on the way to her office, with Jeffrey in front of her in the hallway. "He said something about Amanda and—"

"Unfortunately," Lizzie replied, a chill creeping into her bones, "he's Amanda's father."

* * *

Hank's third trip to the refrigerator didn't net him any more than the first two had. He looked at his watch again. Seven thirty-three. Five minutes later than the last time he'd looked.

Back in the living room, he grabbed his cell phone and checked the messages again. Nothing. And the phone in the apartment hadn't rung all evening.

Why hadn't Lizzie called?

After forcing himself to leave Images, Inc., instead of marching inside to tell the jerk that Lizzie and Amanda were off-limits, and ordering him to leave, Hank returned to work. That had been a mistake. He hadn't been able to keep his mind on anything but what might be happening in Lizzie's office. He had given everyone in the office instructions to tell her to call him at home, if she called, and he had made sure to turn on his voice mail. Nearly five hours later, he was still trying to convince himself there had been a glitch somewhere in the communications system.

Quickly punching in his office number and the voice mail code, he waited. Nothing on it, either.

He tossed the phone onto the sofa and paced to the other side of the room. She had promised to call. Didn't she know how crazy this was making him?

Out of control and unable to stop himself, he punched the back of a nearby chair. Of course she had no idea how this all affected him. He hadn't bothered to tell her his plans. They hadn't had time. She had needed to get back to the office and he had felt the need to make sure he wasn't making a mistake. He hadn't really been sure how he felt until they were on their way back from the park. He had told Daniel that he had decided to stay. He had told him that it was because of Lizzie. He knew what he wanted to happen. He wanted to become a part of her family. Hers and Amanda's. But was that family now going to include the father of her child? First loves often had power long after they had ended. Was that what was now happening? Had Lizzie become overwhelmed with feelings from the past?

The ringing of the phone on the end table jolted him, and he lunged for it. Snatching up the receiver, he was sure it was her. "Look, Lizzie, I—"

"Well, I ain't Lizzie, but I sure hope this is Hank Davis."

The disappointment was almost too much to bear and he sank to the chair, rubbing his eyes. "George?"

"Yep, it's me," his former employer replied. "Wasn't sure if you were still at the number you gave me. Guess you are."

"Yeah. Yeah, I'm still here."

"I'm glad I found you. I was afraid you might not have taken to that new foreman's job and took off for parts unknown without contacting me."

When he got going, George was a talker. Quick-witted and the best boss Hank had ever had, the man was a living, breathing contradiction. His slow amble and speech made one believe his thinking was just as slow. He had won numerous bids on job projects exactly because of that. People often thought he wasn't on the ball. They were wrong.

"I told you I'd let you know if it didn't work out," Hank reminded him. But it had worked out. Much more than he had ever imagined. He liked his job. He was going places with it. Places he had never dreamed possible. He had found a grandfather he hadn't known about or even cared if he did and discovered that he was proud to be Daniel Wallace's grandson. And he had found a woman who was someone special.

"Hank, you still there?"

"I'm here."

After working for the man for three years, Hank knew George well enough to know he didn't talk unless he had something important to say. He might start off with a ramble, but when he got to the point, it was best to be paying attention. Hank was ready to cut to the chase. "What's up, George?"

On the other end of the line, George's quiet chuckle was still audible. "You know me better than anyone else. Except Junie. And she's always one step ahead of me. The thing is, I'm putting the business on the market, Hank. Junie has finally convinced me that all this travelin' is cuttin' down on the time we have left. We're gettin' older, and Junie has this idea that she wants to settle down and live like normal folks. I have to admit I'm of the same mind."

"You're selling GJ Construction?" Hank asked, taken completely by surprise.

"Yep. And I remembered once how you said that if I ever had the urge to close down, you wanted first shot at buying it."

Hank remembered, too. It had been one night after he and George and some of the other guys had shared a few too many pitchers of beer. Many of the other guys had families. One of them had talked at length about missing his wife and kids. Two days later, the guy quit to go back to Colorado to be with his family. Hank had been morose and at loose ends that night. A part of him had always wanted a different life, but another part of him had embraced the life he had with gusto. He and George had talked into the wee hours.

He hadn't thought about that conversation since then, but he needed to give it some thought. Some long thought.

"How much are you asking?"

George named a price that Hank didn't feel was out of range. He could do it. Even though he had spent a chunk of money since moving to Kansas City, he still had a sizable amount in savings. Enough for a down payment. His credit was good. And if he had to, he would go to his grandfather. Daniel might not be wild about Hank leaving, but Hank was sure he would be willing to help.

But did he want to leave? His watch told him that more time had gone by than he felt was necessary for Lizzie to talk to her former lover. Still, he held on to a thread of hope that she had other reasons for not calling.

"Are you in a hurry for an answer?" he asked George, hoping to buy some time.

"A couple of other guys have approached me," George admitted, "and I need to let them know as soon as possible if I'm considering their bids. But I wanted you to have the first chance. I know you'd do GJ a good turn."

Hank considered it. He would be his own boss. The owner of a close-knit company. But there was Crown to consider. And Wallace International. And there was Lizzie, although he didn't have a clue where he stood with her. Especially now.

"How 'bout I call you around ten tonight?" he offered. He didn't want to ignore this opportunity, just in case. And, by that time, Lizzie would have called. Hopefully.

"Sounds fine," George answered.

Hank ended the call and hung up the phone, staring at it and willing it to ring again. It didn't.

Two hours later, Hank hadn't heard from Lizzie. She hadn't returned the two calls he had made to her, and he was losing hope. Now he wondered if it wasn't for the best. He had begun to wonder if he hadn't been fooling himself by thinking he could be a family man. He couldn't deny his love for Lizzie any longer. And he had made a connection with Amanda. On their trip to the zoo, he had had a glimpse of what it would be like to be her father. A flicker of hope had planted itself in his heart that he just might someday have his own family.

But Amanda's father had returned and, whether or not Hank thought he was a jerk, the man was still Amanda's father. What hope did Hank, a virtual outsider and son of a drifter, have of being a father to her?

His decision had been made for him. He would call George and tell him he was interested in buying GJ Construction. They could work out the details later. If he had to ask Daniel for help, he would.

But even though his plans had taken a new direction toward a new life, there was still a small shred of hope that he could salvage a part of the old one. How, he wasn't sure.

Lizzie dumped her purse on the sofa and hurried to where Hank stood near the window. Not caring what he thought, she slipped her arms around his waist and rested her cheek on his broad chest. All she wanted was to feel safe in his arms again. "I'm so sorry I didn't call last night. It was awful."

For a moment, she wondered if he was going to

touch her, but he finally put his hands on her shoulders. It was an odd gesture, considering what she had been through the day before. Even odder after what had happened during their motorcycle ride.

Pulling back, she looked at him. His brown-eyed gaze met hers and panic gripped her heart. "Hank?"

He slid his hands down her arms until he reached behind him. Gently he pulled her hands away, but continued to hold them. "I have some news."

Lizzie couldn't breathe. What could have happened in less than twenty-four hours to change him? The day before, he had touched her with loving hands. Even his words had given her hope. She had carried that hope with her throughout her ordeal with Jeffrey. And now?

Leading her to the sofa, he settled her there, then moved to stand behind a chair. Confusion wrapped itself around her. "What is it? What's happened?" Her own voice sounded strange and foreign, strained and fearful, but she couldn't stop it.

"George Brundy called me last night with an offer."

"George Brundy?"

He nodded. "My old boss in New Mexico."

New Mexico? No, she wouldn't believe a simple phone call from an old boss would make a difference. Not when he had been offered Wallace International. Not when he had found his grandfather. Not when she loved him so much and had allowed herself to dream of a future with him, risking her heart and her daughter's.

"What did he want?" she asked, more fearful of his answer than she had ever been about anything.

"He's selling his company."

She didn't want to hear more. She knew what was coming, but she couldn't think of a way to stop it.

"I'm buying it from him," he continued, without making eye contact with her. "We'll make the arrangements in Gallup, after I talk to Daniel. But I wanted you to know first."

Even though she had expected the worst, it did nothing to ward off the pain of hearing it. The room grayed and she felt herself sway, thankful he had had the good sense to put her on the sofa. Not wanting Hank to see how the news affected her, she sat rigidly on the sofa and prayed she could get through this one last thing before she could slink away and hide forever.

"I see."

Gripping the back of the chair in front of him, he lowered his head. "I thought it might matter to you, but I shouldn't be surprised that it doesn't."

His voice was so low and quiet, she wasn't sure she'd heard him correctly. Should she risk an answer? If she hadn't heard right... "It matters," she said before thinking any more about it. When he looked up at her, she couldn't stop herself. "How can you think it wouldn't?"

"Things have changed. Amanda's father has come back."

She shook her head and stood. "No, not as far as I'm concerned. He wasn't there when I needed him the most. Not from the beginning."

"It's not the past that's important, but the present."

She realized he was using her own words against her. "He's never been a father, Hank. He never will be."

He moved from behind the chair and walked toward her, stopping halfway. "He's Amanda's father, past, present and future. You can't change that."

She walked toward him and stopped within touching distance, but didn't reach out to him. The man was infuriating! Why couldn't he understand? "Jeffrey isn't staying. In fact, he's on his way out of town now. His name isn't on Amanda's birth certificate. He has no legal rights and he knows it would take a long court battle to gain anything. He doesn't want to be a father. He never did. His being here was nothing but a whim. I'm not easily intimidated. Amanda was sleeping and didn't see him. I made it clear to him that he'll never see her. Nothing has changed. Can't you understand that?"

"But he's still her father. Her flesh-and-blood father. No one can take his place. Not for her. And not for you."

"Damm it, Hank. You aren't making sense."

One dark eyebrow raised. "You don't see it from my perspective. You warned me not to do this with Amanda. You warned me not to let her get attached, but I did it my way. Funny thing is, neither of us saw what was coming. It wasn't just how Amanda would feel, it was what would happen to me. You were right. I can't take the place of her father. I'm not her father."

The fight drained out of her. "So it's about Amanda?"

"Only a small part. Mostly it's you. And me. Whether we could be—" He reached out and brushed her cheek with his knuckles. "This isn't what I wanted."

"Then do what you want to do," she said, curling

her hand into his. "Nothing has changed. Not unless we let it."

He shook his head and stepped back, releasing her hold on him, as if breaking some kind of bond. "Do you want me to tell Amanda that I'm leaving, or do you want to?"

Tears stung her eyes, forcing her to turn around so he wouldn't see. She didn't want to go through this again with Amanda, but it was a mother's job, not his. "I'll tell her."

He caressed her arm. "I never wanted to hurt her. Never wanted to...hurt...you."

"I'll survive."

"You understand that this is better, don't you?"

Furious, she spun around. "Better? How can you think that?"

"I'm not a man who can stay in one place for long, Lizzie. You've said so yourself."

"Maybe I was wrong." But when she looked at him, she wasn't even sure of that. The only thing she had been wrong about was letting herself fall in love with him. It was a mistake she wouldn't repeat. Not with anyone. This time she was certain.

With nothing more to say, she walked to the sofa and picked up her purse. There wasn't any reason to stay and argue with a man who let his heart lead him to drift. A man who obviously didn't want her love.

"I'll keep in touch," he said from behind her as she made her way to the door.

"Whatever you want to do," she replied without looking back.

Her hand shook as she reached for the doorknob and turned it. She wasn't certain she was strong enough to step out the door. But she had to, and she did.

As she pulled the door closed behind her, she glanced back at Hank, who stood watching her. He didn't look happy and reminded her of a lost little boy. She wondered if he had fooled himself throughout his life, thinking that being a loner would keep him safe and make him happy. She wondered if she ever would be again.

Chapter Ten

Hank paid the driver and waited until the taxi was almost out of sight before he checked out the construction site. When he did, it was evident that GJ Construction was finishing up on the housing project they'd started before he'd left for Kansas City. Neat houses stood silent and empty in rows, while road graders and cement trucks vied for what would soon be streets. A pickup drove past him, stirring up the red New Mexico dust in its wake. New trees and shrubs crowded the back of it, ready to be planted by the landscapers. It was a familiar sight. One he had seen a hundred times and never failed to give him thought. What would it be like to live in a house like that? With a family of his own.

He shook the thought from his mind. He'd burned his bridges and turned his back on the only possibility for that when he left Kansas City. When he had told Daniel he was leaving, his grandfather had argued. But Hank knew what had to be done and Daniel had eventually accepted it, with a promise from Hank to keep in touch. It was too late to go back.

"Hank? Hank Davis?"

Hank turned around to see one of the crew he had worked with for close to three years. "Hey, Tom," he called out. "How's it going?"

"Well, I'll be damned." Tom grabbed Hank's hand and pumped it while he pounded his back in welcome. "George said you were coming back, but we didn't believe him. Not when he said you were going to buy the business from him."

Sorry that he would no longer be one of the crew, but the boss instead, Hank looked down at the dirt beneath his feet that would someday be green with new grass. "As far as I know, there haven't been any papers signed and no money has exchanged hands," he reminded his friend. "You'll have to ask George."

"George isn't saying much," Tom said with a laugh. "Don't think he wanted to trust it until he saw you back here. The boys'll be glad to hear it. You'll make a mighty fine boss."

Embarrassed, Hank muttered his thanks.

More men began to join them, all wanting to greet Hank and know if the rumor was true. Questions about his time in Kansas City were thrown at him, and he tried to answer as many as he could. He enjoyed being with these men again and soon found himself smiling.

"Find any purty wimmin' there?" one of the older guys, who had been with the company for years, asked.

Hank's smile and good nature vanished. He had no intention of sharing tales of the time he'd had with Lizzie for the sake of male conversation. He had never shared much about women or his life with these men, except for George on one or two occasions. He wouldn't start now. "There wasn't time for women, Saul. I was working."

"Hell, Hank, there's always time fer wimmin'!"

Good-natured laughter surrounded him, and he suddenly wished he wasn't standing among them. To his relief, George stepped out of the site trailer and glowered at them all.

"You men have a job to do," he told them. "Get to it or your next boss will be hiring new men." He turned to Hank. "Come on in, son. They won't get nothin' done if you stay out here. Besides, we have business to talk over."

His statement sent a new wave of speculation through the crew as they wandered back to their work. Hank followed George into the trailer and took a seat on the beat-up chair in front of the desk. He had spent a lot of time there in the past, and it almost felt like home. Almost. He wondered if anyplace ever would. He hadn't even thought about his own dilapidated pull-behind. There wasn't much there that meant anything to him.

George settled behind the desk. "My lawyer is going to meet us at Barney's Place about seven with the papers. I thought maybe we could invite the boys to grab a bite to eat with us there and then celebrate with a few beers afterward."

"Sounds fine," Hank lied. There was an empty hole in him that neither food nor sleep could fill. But he didn't want to think about it. Maybe once the papers were signed, he would head back to his trailer and give alcohol a try. He could drink until he passed out, just like his dad had done so many times after his mother was gone.

The thought brought him up short. He didn't want to turn into a version of his dad. It didn't matter that he didn't have a son or daughter it would affect, or that he would never have a son or daughter at all. He didn't plan to waste the rest of his life with a bottle in his hand and a head full of nothing.

"Dinner sounds good," he said, "but I think I'll skip the beers. Must be jet lag."

"Could be," George said, peering at him across the desk. "You do seem kinda tired." He pushed to his feet. "Let's go tell the crew to meet us at Barney's. You can tell me all about the big city on the way there."

Following George to the door, Hank wondered how he could get out of talking about Kansas City. He had left that chapter of his life behind, much like he'd left so many others. Only this time he couldn't seem to let go, the way he always had before. He hoped time would change that.

Outside, George barked at a group of men. "Get the cleanup done. I don't want to see so much as a roofing nail tomorrow morning when the new owner takes over." He turned to grin at Hank before continuing his orders. "When you're done, meet us at Barney's for some barbecue. I'm buyin'."

The whoops and hollers of the men followed them to George's pickup, and Hank climbed in, almost smiling. It would be different being the boss of these men who had been his friends and co-workers. He hoped he could pull it off.

The scenery sped by as George drove them to the restaurant, talking all the while about the plans he and

Junie had made since Hank had accepted the offer. Hank did his best to keep up with the conversation, nodding and making the right noises when it was expected, but not really listening.

At the restaurant, George warned the owner about the crowd that would be joining them, then they found a group of empty tables in the back. Sitting down, Hank felt like he'd been rode hard and left to dry.

"So who's this Daniel fella you mentioned?" George asked, after the waitress had left a pitcher of beer and two glasses on the table.

"My grandfather."

George looked up from the beer he was pouring. "You mean you found some family? I'll be damned. What's he like?"

"Rich," Hank replied, without thinking.

George stared at him while he mopped up the spilled beer on the tabletop. "Rich? No wonder you have the money to buy GJ."

Shaking his head, Hank frowned. "His money isn't buying it. Mine is."

"Yeah, you haven't had many expenses. Drifters like you seldom do."

The word sent a cold chill up Hank's spine. He didn't want to be a drifter. He wanted more. And he'd been dumb enough to throw his chance away.

"I need to make a call," he said, pushing his chair back and getting to his feet. Stuffing his hand into the pocket of his jeans, he realized he didn't have anything smaller than a fifty-dollar bill and wished he'd kept the cell phone Lizzie had given him. He pulled out a bill and tossed it at George. "Can you give me some change for the phone?"

George stared at the bill, then dug in his pocket

and came up with a handful of coins. Hank wasn't sure it would be enough and hoped he could get more at the register if he needed it.

By the time he reached the pay phone hanging on the wall, his palms were sweating. What if Lizzie wouldn't talk to him? She hadn't been all that friendly when he'd called her before he left. But if he didn't try, just one more time, he'd kick himself into the next millennium.

He nearly dropped the coins as he stuffed them into the phone and muttered a curse for being nervous. Taking a deep breath, he dialed the familiar number. It rang once. Twice. Three times. On the fourth, her voice mail picked up. Not wanting to leave a message, he hung up.

Instead of returning to the table, he picked up the receiver again, shoved more money into the phone and dialed Daniel's number. On the third ring, Martha answered.

"Is my grandfather in?" he asked.

"Hank? Is that you? Gracious me, it's good to hear from you. Just a minute. I'll get Daniel."

Hank waited, wondering what had possessed him to call his grandfather. But maybe Daniel had talked to Lizzie. Hank only wanted to make sure she was okay. *Yeah, right.*

"Hank? Where are you?"

"In one of the world's greatest barbecue places."

"In Kansas City?"

Closing his eyes, Hank swallowed the lump in his throat. He suddenly realized he had not only walked out on Lizzie, but he'd disappointed Daniel, his only family. "No. Gallup. I just wondered... Well, I tried to call Lizzie, but she wasn't home. Have you talked to her lately?"

Daniel didn't answer immediately. "Lizzie?"

Before Daniel said more, Hank heard a shriek in the background. And that shriek belonged to Amanda. "Are they there? Lizzie and Amanda?"

"As a matter of fact they are," Daniel said, his pride evident in the tone of his voice. "They've come to keep an old man company and make him feel young, if even for a little while." He was silent for a moment again. "Do you want to talk to Lizzie?"

Suddenly Hank couldn't think of why he had wanted to talk to her. He could hear Amanda's giggles in the background, and could have sworn he heard some kind of yipping noise. Nobody was missing him. People just went on with their lives. Even those he loved the most.

"She's right here," Daniel was saying.

"No! I mean, I only wanted to know if she's all—"

"Hello, Hank."

"Lizzie."

"How's New Mexico?"

He could hear the tension in her voice and wondered if Daniel had shoved the phone into her hand. "Same as always."

"Oh."

Nerves made him tongue-tied. There wasn't any reason why he couldn't just talk to her like he normally did. "I hear Amanda. What's she doing?"

She gave a nervous little laugh. "Oh, she talked me into getting a puppy. Only I'm afraid she won't be a puppy for long."

"Yeah? I bet she's having the time of her life."

"Well, you know how much she likes animals."

He knew they were both remembering their trip to the zoo and he couldn't think of a blasted thing to say. "Everything else okay?"

"Yes, just fine."

The cheer in her voice was forced, and he didn't think he could take any more. "Tell Amanda I miss her."

"I will."

He had to say it. He couldn't just say goodbye and not tell her. "And, Lizzie?" He tried to say it. Tried to say the words he needed to say. But he couldn't. "I miss you, too," he said instead.

He heard a strange, soft sound, then nothing.

"She had to go take care of something," Daniel said on the other end.

Feeling as if he'd been kicked, Hank was ready to end the conversation. He could hear the censure in Daniel's voice. It wasn't nearly as bad as what he thought of himself. "I'll talk to you later in the week," he told his grandfather. "Looks like the ribs are here."

But the ribs didn't look at all appetizing, especially when George introduced him to the man in the suit, who had joined them.

"Jack Nolan, my attorney," George said as Hank shook hands with the man. "Why don't you join us for some barbecue, Jack?"

The man shook his head. "I'd love to, but my wife's parents are due for dinner. If we could just get to the paperwork..."

Hank listened as Nolan explained the details of the sale contract. Or tried to listen. The funny sound he'd heard on the phone kept nagging at him. The more he thought about it, the more it sounded like Lizzie was crying. And it was his fault. All his fault.

"If you'll just sign here," Nolan said, pointing to the signature line on the paper.

Hank took the pen from him and bent over, ready to put his name on the paper. He stared at it. Owning GJ Construction had at one time been a lofty dream, back when he thought he'd never be much of anything. But he'd done more than that during his short time in Kansas City. He had proven that he knew more about the business of construction than he had thought. More about business in general. And he wanted to learn more. There were dozens of things he had wanted to do with Wallace International. Things that would make it even better than Daniel had made it.

But more than anything, he wanted a family. His family. Lizzie and Amanda. So what if Jeffrey was Amanda's father? Hank had been more of a father than Jeffrey had ever thought of being. And Hank was pretty sure he could be a much better one.

Straightening, he handed the pen to George. "I'm sorry, but I can't do it. Tell Junie I'm sorry."

"What—" George began.

"You can find another buyer, can't you?"

"Well, I don't—"

"Then I'll buy it for Crown." Hank took the pen from George and quickly scribbled his signature.

"Crown? How can you—"

"Daniel Wallace is my grandfather." Hank tossed the pen on the table and pulled four fifties from his wallet. "Tell the crew it's on me. And tell them I'll make sure they have a good foreman."

"But, Daniel Wallace?" George asked as Hank

walked away. "Doesn't he own Wallace International?"

Hank didn't bother to answer. He had other things to say to somebody else. Just as soon as he could catch a flight back to Kansas City.

"Do you know where she is?"

Bailey looked in the rearview mirror of the limo and grinned. "Sure. It took some work, but I found her and, by my guess, she'll be there for a while."

Hank let out a long sigh of relief and leaned back against the leather seat. "Good. I probably made a mess of your plans for today, but you were the only person I knew who might be able to help. I owe you one."

"Not me," Bailey replied. "I'm glad to do it."

Hank smiled his thanks and closed his eyes. It had been a wild night. Because George had been in a hurry to sell, Hank had put his motorcycle in storage in Kansas City. He was completely without transportation in New Mexico to get back to the construction site where his trailer and old pickup were still parked. As he was leaving Barney's the night before, and trying to figure out how to get everything done that needed doing, the crew had arrived and Tom offered to lend a hand. They'd been too late to find a flight back to Kansas City until today, but they had gotten a lot done. Knowing he wouldn't be returning to New Mexico, no matter what happened with Lizzie, they packed what was left of his belongings, and Tom promised to take care of the empty trailer. When Hank had a flight number, he called Bailey and asked him to find Lizzie and keep tabs on her. Bailey agreed to do that and to pick him up at the airport.

Now all Hank had to do was convince Lizzie of how sorry he was for everything and that he would never leave her again. Considering he hadn't acted like a man who wanted permanence in his life, he knew that might be a tall order.

When the limo pulled into the gravel driveway in front of Daniel's home, Hank wasn't sure he would be able to do it. He had never given her reason to believe he wouldn't take off when the mood struck him. But he knew he wouldn't and, in time, he would prove it to her. Even if it took a lifetime.

The limo came to a stop and Bailey got out to open the rear door for Hank. "Yeah, I know," he said with a grin. "I'm not supposed to do this. But it's for luck, you know?"

Hank climbed out and took his outstretched hand to shake it. "Thanks. I have a feeling I'm going to need it."

"I'll stay here until I hear from you."

Nodding, Hank thanked him again, then started up the walk toward the house. With each step, his mouth went a little drier. He wasn't sure what kind of welcome he might get from Lizzie, or from his grandfather. They might both send him on his way. But if they did, it would only make him more determined.

After ringing the bell, he waited. Several long seconds later, the door opened to reveal Martha. The look on her face didn't give him much hope.

She crossed her arms on her ample chest. "So. You're back."

"I'm back to stay, Martha."

"No more running off? You're ready to settle down?"

"More than ready."

A smile lit her face. "I'm glad."

Relieved, he returned the smile. "Me, too."

"Daniel and Lizzie are out back," she said, ushering him into the entryway. "Amanda is having the time of her life with that puppy and wearing them both out."

Hank followed her through the house and into the oversize kitchen. Through the open doorway, he could see Lizzie attempting to teach a ball of fur a few manners.

Martha stopped him before he could step outside. "It's good to know you have more common sense than your mother did, God rest her soul, but I won't see Daniel hurt again. Or Lizzie and that little girl, either, for that matter."

"If they get hurt, it won't be because of me. I promise."

She gave him a motherly hug, then shooed him out the door, dabbing at her eyes with the end of her apron.

Standing on the patio, Hank watched the scene before him. Lizzie sat on the lush carpet of grass, laughing while Amanda tumbled with a puppy that was more than half her size. Hank smiled, knowing the dog would be bigger than her in no time. His grandfather was bent over a rosebush with a pair of pruning sheers. Hank's heart filled with an emotion he recognized as love. He wanted nothing more in life than to be a part of this family.

Lizzie turned and looked up. Even from a distance, he heard her gasp of surprise and saw her eyes widen. Scrambling to her feet, she brushed the grass from her blue jeans, then stood staring at him.

Daniel must have heard her, too, because he

straightened and turned. A scowl appeared on his face. "Something happen in Gallup?"

"You could say that," Hank answered, thinking of how long it had taken him to discover what it was he really wanted in his life.

Amanda stopped playing with her puppy and squealed with delight when she spied Hank. "You're back! I told Mommy you wouldn't stay away."

"I couldn't stay away if I wanted to," Hank told her when she ran to him. Scooping her into his arms, he nuzzled her neck, producing a giggle. He gave her a hug, then set her on her feet. "I need to talk to your mommy, and then you can introduce me to your puppy, okay?"

Her face solemn, she nodded. "You aren't going to leave again, are you?"

The lost look in her eyes nearly broke his heart. "No. Not ever."

He looked up to see Lizzie walking toward him and moved to meet her. Her face was pale and, the closer he got, he could see dark circles under her eyes. She stopped, not more than a foot from him, her lips set in a tight, unsmiling line.

"Did you forget something?" she asked.

"As a matter of fact, I did." Not eager for Daniel and Amanda to hear what he had to say, he grabbed her hand and started walking to a small gazebo tucked in the corner of the expansive lawn where they could have some privacy. She attempted to pull away from him, but he held tight. "You know, if you don't come willingly, I'll have to pick you up and carry you."

She continued to tug at his hand, until he was practically dragging her. Stopping, he bent to scoop her up and placed her as gently as possible over his shoulder. "I have something to say, and you're going to listen."

Behind him, he could hear Amanda's giggles and hoped their audience would find something else to do. Until he and Lizzie talked—until he could tell her what he hadn't been able to tell her before—he wanted her all to himself.

"Put me down, Hank," she demanded. "You're making a scene."

"Nope. I don't want you running off." Taking care on the steps leading into the gazebo, he ducked inside and slipped her off his shoulder, enjoying the feel of her sliding against him.

"You were the one who ran off," she reminded him, stepping back.

"And now you're doing the same." He fought the urge to reach out and touch her. "Don't do it, Lizzie. Just listen to me."

"Do I have a choice?"

With the frown she wore and the stubborn tilt of her chin, he had his work cut out for him. "As a matter of fact, you don't." When she didn't answer, he went on, determined to break down the wall between them, even if it was bit by bit. "I want a new contract drawn up."

For a moment, she didn't move, then she shook her head. "I'm sorry. I'm not taking on any new clients. Images, Inc., is booked for several months."

"Not that kind of contract," he said, locking his gaze with hers.

"You can't keep doing this to Amanda," she said, her eyes filling with tears. "Or to me."

Unable to stop himself, he reached for her to slide his hands up and down her arms. More than anything, he wanted to hold her, but he knew she wouldn't stand for that. Not yet. "I won't."

"What is it you want, Hank?"

"A contract." When she started to turn away from him, he held her and kept her from moving. "Between you and me. I'm here to stay, whether you want me or not. You're what I've been searching for."

She leaned back and stared at him, a guarded look in her eyes. "I—I am?"

He nodded. "I want a marriage contract. I love you, Lizzie. It isn't what I planned, but I'm not going to fight it anymore. I want us to be a family. You and me and Amanda. And the babies we'll have in the future. I want to be Amanda's father, but more than that, I want to be your love. I won't leave you, I swear. I'm here forever."

Her eyes glittered with a mixture of love and tears. "Oh, Hank, I love you—"

Before she could finish, he pulled her close and crushed her lips with his. She wound her arms around his neck and clung to him, returning his kiss with so much love, she took his breath away.

"What the—" he muttered against her lips. Regretfully loosening his hold on the woman who had taught him how to love, he looked down to see the ball of fur jumping furiously at them. "Damned animal is going to eat us out of house and home," he said, bending over to scratch the puppy's ears.

"Images, Inc., is doing very well. I don't think we'll have to worry about it," Lizzie said, laughing.

He straightened. "Images, Inc., won't have to worry about it. I guess Wallace International can keep us in dog food."

"Then you're going to accept Daniel's offer? What about the construction company in New Mexico?"

"If Daniel is agreeable, GJ can become a part of Crown. It's a good, solid company, and I have an idea of who can oversee it," he said, thinking of how Tom had unselfishly come to his aid.

"Daniel will be pleased."

Hank slipped an arm around Lizzie's waist and maneuvered them around the pup. Leading her outside, he could see Amanda and Daniel waiting in the distance. "I'd better tell him."

"Mommy, why were you kissing Hank?" Amanda asked when they neared the pair.

Lizzie looked at Hank, her eyes glowing with happiness. "Because I love him."

Amanda wrapped her arms around the two of them. "I love bofe of you!" Tail wagging, the puppy attacked her with a wet tongue, covering her face in doggy kisses when she bent down to pet her. "And I love Penelope, too!"

While they watched the child and the puppy play, Daniel approached them. "I see you two have reached an agreement. I hope it means you'll be staying here in Kansas City."

Lizzie looked up at Hank, love shining in her eyes, and his heart nearly burst with the joy of it. "We wouldn't think of leaving here," Hank told his grandfather, as he pulled Lizzie closer. "I hope your offer is still open, but if it isn't, I'm content to stay where I am."

Daniel's eyes sparkled with happiness and he reached out to take Hank's hand. "Of course it's still open. I never closed it. You're the only one I'd trust with my companies."

Nodding, Lizzie smiled first at Daniel, then at Hank. "It's your legacy, Hank. You finally have your family."

Hank felt an unaccustomed peace. Not only did he have his grandfather for family, but soon there would be more, and they would be his own. It wasn't simply a family legacy, but a legacy of love.

Epilogue

"Martha, I think we can bring out the potato salad and bread now," Lizzie's mother said. "It looks like everyone is about ready to eat."

Standing on the edge of the patio, out of the way, Hank smiled at Martha as she passed him on her way into Daniel's kitchen. A trail of brown balls of fur followed her.

"Penelope!" Dean shouted at the dog. "Get over here and tend to your offspring before they trip somebody and all the food ends up on the ground."

"I think that's their plan," Hank told him as he helped gather the litter of puppies and returned them to the portable kennel Lizzie had insisted they bring along. "Crazy women, putting dogs in a playpen."

"And Christmas trees," Dean agreed.

"And clean laundry," Hank added, laughing.

"But never a baby," Dean said, scooping up his two-and-a-half-year-old daughter who was intent on following the puppies. She wiggled and whimpered to get down, then as soon as he set her on her feet, she rushed to the kennel to poke her fingers in for puppy licks.

Amanda came to the rescue. "Come on, Ginny, let's go try the new swings Grandpa Dan made." She turned to Hank. "Can James swing too? Grandpa Dan made two baby swings."

Hank nodded. "I'll bet your little brother would like that. Just be sure to keep an eye on him. Maybe Roger and Denny can help."

With Ginny in tow, Amanda went searching for her toddler brother. Hank watched her, still amazed at how she had accepted him three years ago as her father and made sure everyone was aware of it. The adoption papers had been rushed through the courts, thanks to Daniel's connections, making him her legal father. And if he knew her as well as he thought he did, she would have Roger and Denny charmed into being her slaves for the day. Her strawberry-blond ponytail bounced at her neck, and he noticed how she swayed her hips, just like her mother, when she was trying to be grown-up. He shook his head, chuckling quietly. He would have to keep his eye on her as she got older. Boys would be knocking down the door, especially those hoping to get in good with the CEO of Wallace International. But she would never have to worry that he, or even Daniel, would let history repeat itself. They had both learned their lesson about pride.

"What are you laughing at now?" Lizzie asked, slipping her arms around him from behind. "Bailey and Janine?"

He scanned the yard until he found the pair she'd mentioned, their heads together and their hands entwined, trying to slip away to the gazebo for a few minutes of privacy before lunchtime. With his small fleet of limousines, Bailey was becoming quite a businessman and a good catch for any woman. "No, but now that you mention it, someone should warn them about that gazebo."

Lizzie leaned around him to look at him. "Why? Because it was where we finally came to our senses and you proposed? Maybe it's enchanted?"

"Not as enchanting as you," Hank whispered, reaching back to capture a long tendril of her loose hair. Wrapping his fingers in it, he pulled her around to face him. "I never thought things could get any better than they were that day, but they have. Every day."

Stepping into the circle of his arms, she rested her head on his chest. "For all of us."

"And more of us." Slipping his hand between them, he gently caressed her growing belly. "We've almost caught up with Vicky and Dean."

"Time to eat," Mrs. Edwards called to the family.

Lizzie moved as if to join them, but Hank kept her close, and together they watched as the others began to gather at the long picnic table across the patio. "Quite a family, isn't it?" she said, her voice filled with pride.

"The best," he said, thinking of the love they all shared. "And I'm lucky to be a part of it."

"I'm the lucky one. I have you." She stood on tiptoe to kiss his cheek. "Come on," she said, tugging at him. "We'd better find a seat before everything is gone."

"With all that food?" He hung back, teasing her

with his protest. "And what's with Daniel and Martha and Mom?"

"Oh, he's loving every bit of the attention."

"Look at that. I half expect to see Mom tuck a napkin under his chin while Martha cuts his food. Maybe I should have a talk with him."

"Maybe you should let them enjoy themselves."

With another tug from Lizzie, he moved his feet in the direction of the table. "When do *we* get to enjoy ourselves?" he whispered in her ear.

"When we get home," she promised with a tempting smile. "Which reminds me, I need to talk to Janine about our newest class. Images, Inc., has grown so much, we need more help. I thought we might try a mentoring program with some of the kids who have been clients."

"If it would mean more time for us to be together, I'm all for it." He had never been more proud than the day she had received her master's degree in psychology and started a program for high school students in need of building self-esteem. But it had all meant she never got around to cutting back her hours.

"I'd say we've managed to have some time together," she replied, placing her hand on the roundness where their newest family member grew. "Very much more time and we'll have our own basketball team."

He grinned at her. "There's plenty of room for that."

"But not at the table." She picked up James and put him in his high chair next to Ginny at the end of the table.

When they had all taken their places, Daniel quieted them by standing at the other end. "I don't believe I've ever felt so blessed." He smiled at the ladies—one to his left, the other to his right—then at the rest of the family, seated around the table, which was loaded with picnic fare. "For too many years, I lived alone. I never realized how much I missed the sounds of children playing, but now that I have my great-grandchildren and another on the way, I want this house to always be filled with laughter. To accomplish that, I've given Hank and Lizzie the property."

Hank heard Lizzie's small gasp of surprise. Leaning closer to him, she whispered, "Did you know about this?"

"Daniel and I talked about it."

"But where—"

"Shh. Listen."

Daniel continued. "Although I'm enjoying my retirement, now that Hank has taken over the reins of Wallace International—and doing a fine job of it, without me," he added with a fake scowl he quickly replaced with a smile, "I had considered moving to Florida. But I can't leave my family, now that I have you all. Instead I've arranged, with the help of the CEO, for Crown Construction to build a retirement center."

"Oh, Daniel, that's wonderful!" Martha said.

"Here in Kansas City?" Mrs. Edwards asked. "Put my name on the list, Daniel."

"Hank gets the credit for the idea," Daniel said, with a nod toward his grandson. "You can get the details from him."

Amid the chorus of congratulations and eager questions, Hank caught Lizzie studying him. "What's wrong?" he asked, concerned by the touch of sadness he saw in her eyes.

"It's wonderful. I can't imagine living here." She moved to look past him at the house behind them. "Only... I was wondering what would have happened to you and your parents if things had been different."

Slipping his arm around her and pulling her close, he kissed her temple. "That's the past, and we'll never know what might have been. But I wouldn't trade it if it meant we wouldn't have met. No matter where we are, no matter where we live, as long as we have each other, we'll be a family."

He placed his hand on her firm, round belly, and said a silent thank-you for the woman who had given him a family and taught him how to love. If it hadn't been for her, he might never have known true happiness.

The past was behind them, the future ahead, and the present was more than he had ever dreamed possible.

* * * * *

SILHOUETTE Romance®

In May 2003, experience a story that'll both tug at your heartstrings and cause you to laugh out loud— from one of Silhouette Romance's most beloved authors,

MELISSA McCLONE!

What do you get when you trap a sexy businessman and a breathtaking heiress on a tropical island and force them to compete for a grand prize? A steamy attraction that's bound to turn into...

The Wedding Adventure
(#1661)

Available at your favorite retail outlet

Silhouette®
Where love comes alive™

Visit Silhouette at www.eHarlequin.com

SRTWA

eHARLEQUIN.com

Becoming an eHarlequin.com member is easy, fun and **FREE!** Join today to enjoy great benefits:

- **Super savings** on all our books, including members-only discounts and offers!
- Enjoy **exclusive online reads**—FREE!
- Info, tips and **expert advice** on writing your own romance novel.
- FREE romance **newsletters,** customized by you!
- Find out the latest on your **favorite authors.**
- Enter to win exciting **contests and promotions!**
- Chat with other members in our **community message boards!**

Plus, we'll send you 2 FREE Internet-exclusive eHarlequin.com books (no strings!) just to say thanks for joining us online.

To become a member, visit www.eHarlequin.com today!

INTMEMB

If you enjoyed what you just read,
then we've got an offer you can't resist!

Take 2 bestselling love stories FREE!

Plus get a FREE surprise gift!

Clip this page and mail it to Silhouette Reader Service™

IN U.S.A.	IN CANADA
3010 Walden Ave.	P.O. Box 609
P.O. Box 1867	Fort Erie, Ontario
Buffalo, N.Y. 14240-1867	L2A 5X3

YES! Please send me 2 free Silhouette Romance® novels and my free surprise gift. After receiving them, if I don't wish to receive anymore, I can return the shipping statement marked cancel. If I don't cancel, I will receive 6 brand-new novels every month, before they're available in stores! In the U.S.A., bill me at the bargain price of $3.34 plus 25¢ shipping and handling per book and applicable sales tax, if any*. In Canada, bill me at the bargain price of $3.80 plus 25¢ shipping and handling per book and applicable taxes**. That's the complete price and a savings of at least 10% off the cover prices—what a great deal! I understand that accepting the 2 free books and gift places me under no obligation ever to buy any books. I can always return a shipment and cancel at any time. Even if I never buy another book from Silhouette, the 2 free books and gift are mine to keep forever.

215 SDN DNUM
315 SDN DNUN

Name	(PLEASE PRINT)	
Address	Apt.#	
City	State/Prov.	Zip/Postal Code

* Terms and prices subject to change without notice. Sales tax applicable in N.Y.
** Canadian residents will be charged applicable provincial taxes and GST.
All orders subject to approval. Offer limited to one per household and not valid to current Silhouette Romance® subscribers.
® are registered trademarks of Harlequin Books S.A., used under license.

SROM02 ©1998 Harlequin Enterprises Limited

Coming next month from

SILHOUETTE Romance®

Daycare DADS

She can teach him how to raise a child, but what about love...?

Introducing the amazing new series from

SUSAN MEIER

about single fathers needing to learn the ABCs of TLC and the special women up to the challenge.

BABY ON BOARD
January 2003

THE TYCOON'S DOUBLE TROUBLE
March 2003

THE NANNY SOLUTION
May 2003

You won't want to miss a single one!

Visit Silhouette at www.eHarlequin.com

SRDC

Coming in May 2003 from

SILHOUETTE *Romance*®

a very special love story from reader favorite

LAUREY BRIGHT

With His Kiss (#1660)
On sale May 2003

Forced into a business partnership, former adversaries Triss Allerdyce and Steve Stevens wonder how on earth they will be able to work together. Soon, though, their old feuding ways give way to trust—and desire. Can they forgive and forget...and give in to passion?

Available at your favorite retail outlet.

Only from Silhouette Books!

Visit Silhouette at www.eHarlequin.com

SRWHK

COMING NEXT MONTH

#1660 WITH HIS KISS—Laurey Bright

He was back in town! Gunther "Steve" Stevens had always unsettled Triss Allerdyce—and he'd been secretly jealous of her marriage to his much older mentor. But now her husband's will brought them together again, and Steve's anger soon turned to love. But would that be enough to awaken the hidden passions of this Sleeping Beauty?

#1661 THE WEDDING ADVENTURE—Melissa McClone

The *last* thing Cade Armstrong Waters wanted to do was spend two weeks on a tropical island with socialite Cynthia Sterling! But with his charity organization at stake, he agreed to the crazy scheme. Surviving Cynthia's passionate kisses with his heart intact was another story....

#1662 THE NANNY SOLUTION—Susan Meier

Daycare Dads

Nanny Hannah Evans was going to give millionaire Jake Malloy a piece of her mind! It was bad enough the sexy single father was running around like a government spy, but now she was actually falling for her confounding boss. Was he *ever* going to give up his secret double life for fatherhood and...love?

#1663 THE KNIGHT'S KISS—Nicole Burnham

Soulmates

Thanks to a medieval curse, Nick Black had been around for a long time...a *long* time. Researching ancient artifacts for Princess Isabella diTalora, he hoped to find the answers to break the spell. But would he find the one woman who could break the walls around his heart?

#1664 CAPTIVATING A COWBOY—Jill Limber

So city girl Julie Kerns broke her collarbone trying to fix up her grandmother's cottage—she could *hire* someone to help, right? But what if he was ex-Navy SEAL Tony Graham—a man sexy as sin who kissed like heaven? Maybe that cottage would need *a lot* more work than she first thought....

#1665 THE BACHELOR CHRONICLES—Lissa Manley

Jared Warfield was torn between his pride in his business and the need for privacy to adopt his orphaned baby niece. So he planned to show fiesty reporter Erin James all about the store—and nothing about himself. But the best-laid plans went awry when the unlikely couple finally met!